Jo perched on the farthest edge of the tartan blanket that she could, but it made no difference when Taylor joined her, his body and long legs dominating the space.

So much so that his thigh was touching hers, and she could feel his body heat through the thin fabric of her dress. Despite being out of the direct sun, her skin became feverish. It was the closest she'd been to a man since the breakup. That was the only reason she was responding the way she was. It had absolutely nothing to do with the muscular thigh pressed intimately against her leg.

"Jo?"

"Hmm?"

"I was just asking if you'd like a drink." Taylor was looking at her with amusement, and she realized she'd been so caught up in her body's physical reaction to him, and what it meant, that she hadn't heard the question.

"Sorry. I was miles away. Yes, I'd love a drink of lemonade. Thank you." She just needed something to cool down the heat of her embarrassment. The last thing she needed was to find herself attracted to the billionaire who clearly despised her.

T0284414

Dear Reader,

New Year's at our house is usually a quiet family affair. Some food, a toast at midnight and we're in bed about ten minutes later.

When Jo Kirkham gets the chance to celebrate in style, she jumps at it. Caring for her patient over the holidays seems a small price to pay when she's afforded the luxury of spending time on a private island with the wealthy Stroud family. But she hadn't counted on the arrival of prodigal son Taylor, who clearly has an axe to grind...

Join the celebrations, and the emotional journey, with Jo and Taylor, and get carried away to paradise.

Happy New Year!

Karin xx

NURSE'S NEW YEAR WITH THE BILLIONAIRE

KARIN BAINE

MEDICAL ROMANCE

Harlequin®
MEDICAL ROMANCE

Recycling programs for this product may not exist in your area.

ISBN-13: 978-1-335-94270-8

Nurse's New Year with the Billionaire

Copyright © 2024 by Karin Baine

Harlequin Enterprises ULC
22 Adelaide St. West, 41st Floor
Toronto, Ontario M5H 4E3, Canada
www.Harlequin.com

Printed in U.S.A.

Karin Baine lives in Northern Ireland with her husband, two sons and her out-of-control notebook collection. Her mother and her grandmother's vast collection of books inspired her love of reading and her dream of becoming a Harlequin author. Now she can tell people she has a *proper* job! You can follow Karin on X @karinbaine1 or visit her website for the latest news, karinbaine.com.

Books by Karin Baine

Harlequin Medical Romance

Carey Cove Midwives

Festive Fling to Forever

Christmas North and South

Festive Fling with the Surgeon

Royal Docs

Surgeon Prince's Fake Fiancée
A Mother for His Little Princess

A GP to Steal His Heart
Single Dad for the Heart Doctor
Falling Again for the Surgeon
Nurse's Risk with the Rebel
An American Doctor in Ireland
Midwife's One-Night Baby Surprise

Visit the Author Profile page
at Harlequin.com for more titles.

This one is for Keith and Matthew because
apparently they haven't had one yet...

**Praise for
Karin Baine**

"Emotionally enchanting! The story was fast-paced,
emotionally charged and oh so satisfying!"
—*Goodreads* on *Their One-Night Twin Surprise*

CHAPTER ONE

Jo Kirkham closed her eyes, clenched her fists and prayed she wouldn't die.

'I never get used to this either.' Isabelle Stroud, the reason she was on this tiny seaplane imagining plummeting to her death, gently patted her on the knee and did her best to put Jo at ease.

It wasn't working. Being flown out on a private jet with all the privileges and luxuries of working for a wealthy family was entirely different to island hopping in a contraption where she was way too close to the cockpit. The one consolation was that Bensak, the private island owned by Isabelle's entrepreneur son, wasn't too far away.

She never would have dreamed she'd willingly spend Christmas Day travelling, arriving at her destination late on Boxing Day, completely missing the usual festive celebrations. But a free trip to the Fijian islands was the best thing that had happened to her in a long time.

Politeness forced her to open her eyes to address the elderly woman she was here to take care of for the duration of their stay. 'I've only ever flown commercial. This is all new to me.'

Isabelle was recovering from a stroke and Jo had been employed as her private nurse to continue her treatment; making sure she took her medication, keeping an eye on her blood pressure and blood sugar and helping her with her physiotherapy in between appointments. All to try and prevent another stroke from occurring. Her patient was recovering well, with only her mobility still providing a cause for concern, but she might not be so lucky the next time.

The plane hit a pocket of air and bumped them in their seats. Jo bit back a panicked scream and dug her nails deeper into her palms.

'Believe it or not I wasn't on an airplane until I was fifty-four years old,' Isabelle confided, her light blue eyes sparkling at the memory.

'Really?' With the billions the family were reputed to have, Jo imagined fleets of all manner of vehicles at their disposal. Able to transport them anywhere in the world at a moment's notice. A far cry from the daily commute, sardined onto the train with all the other minions whose livelihoods depended on working for rich overseers.

Not that the Stroud family were her sole employers. As a private nurse she took work with whoever needed her, and looking after Isabelle so far had been a joy rather than a chore. Of course, she still had to provide essential medical assistance, which put a great deal of responsibility on her shoulders, but this particular job had its perks. Like accompanying her charge out to the family's private island for New Year's Eve celebrations in a few days.

'We had to work hard for our money. My husband, John, built the business up from the ground and it was years before we were able to take a holiday abroad. It was my son who completely transformed the company and made it what it is today. I've been lucky enough to see the benefits of that. Unfortunately, John didn't live long enough to see Stroud Technologies become the phenomenon it is now. I only wish he were here with me to enjoy all of this. He'd be proud of Paul and everything he has achieved.' She gestured out the window to where the island was coming into view in the midst of the turquoise waters. Paradise.

'I'm sure he would be.' Jo reached across her seat and gave Isabelle's fragile hand a gentle squeeze.

Paul Stroud wasn't just a successful businessman; he was an inventor. Creating all sorts of innovative, and expensive, electrical products that made Stroud Technologies a household name. As well as making the family their fortune.

Isabelle offered her a watery smile. Although they came from completely different worlds, sometimes it felt as though they were more than nurse and patient. She might only have been working with her for a couple of months, but there was a genuine connection between them, and Isabelle had been as beneficial in assisting Jo in recovering from her troubles, as Jo had been in Isabelle's stroke aftercare.

These last couple of years had been tough. Once upon a time, Jo had run her own business with her partner, Steve, providing agency nurses and healthcare assistants to private clients. She'd worked as a nurse herself before starting the business and built it into a successful agency, which afforded her a beautiful big house, where she'd lived with Steve and looked forward to a happy future with him.

Now she was bankrupt, back living with her parents with whom she had a strained relationship to say the least, and was spending the holidays working so she could afford to rent a flat the size of a matchbox. All because Steve had emptied their joint account and fled the country, leaving her behind to face all the unpaid bills and deal with the fallout. He'd broken her spirit as well as her heart, and it had taken her a long time to crawl back out of the black pit of despair he'd tossed her into.

Still, she was taking one day at a time, and today's view was stunning.

'Brace yourselves,' the pilot told them just before they came down with a bump and a splash, and Jo gave a silent prayer of thanks for their safe arrival.

'It looks as though we have a welcome committee.' Isabelle waved out the window to the family members already assembled and awaiting their arrival. They'd flown out ahead, leaving Jo to accompany Isabelle.

She'd be lying if she said she wasn't a little apprehensive. Although she'd met some of the family members, spent a lot of time in Isabelle's home, being part of this gathering was out of her comfort zone. She hadn't been very sociable since her ex had ruined her life, and these were people who moved in some serious social circles. As she escorted Isabelle down onto the golden sand she had to pinch herself that she was here at all.

'Welcome to Bensak Island.' Paul greeted them with open arms, wearing an open-necked white cotton shirt and loose white cotton trousers, looking every inch like the head of a hippy commune. Barefoot, long haired and donning the requisite leather thong necklace, he was either going through some belated mid-life crisis, or he was beginning to believe his own hype. He was the leader of his kingdom on this island.

But Jo couldn't deny his generosity or hospitality.

'Thanks,' she said, dodging the kiss he tried to plant on her lips so he came into contact with her cheek instead.

'Mother.' He met Isabelle with double kisses, but she batted him away.

'It's getting late. Just take us to our rooms, Paul. I'm tired.'

He looked a tad crestfallen by her dismissal, but Jo had been with her patient long enough to know that her crotchetiness was often due to her arthritis. The long journey to get here, not to mention the cramped confines of their last mode of transport, would have taken their toll on the elderly lady's frail body.

'I should probably get your mother settled for the night. It's been a long day.' Jo tried to take some of the sting out of the moment, and Paul immediately perked up.

'Of course. I'll get someone to take you to your quarters.' With a snap of his fingers he summoned what looked like a glorified golf buggy to take them to their accommodation.

Whilst the journey there wasn't smooth, it was worth it to reach their destination. A sprawling, glass-fronted mansion, which appeared to stretch for ever appeared in the midst of the green landscape.

'My son doesn't do understated,' Isabelle mused upon seeing Jo's reaction.

She'd heard about this place, the celebrities and rumoured royals who'd stayed and partied here over the years, but it was something else seeing it materialise like a mirage before her. Knowing this was going to be her home for the next week.

'I'll show you to your rooms and have someone bring you dinner. You can catch up with everyone tomorrow after a good night's sleep.' Paul jumped out of the cart that drew up alongside them and helped his mother out.

'That's okay, Mr Stroud. I'm here in a work capacity to take care of your mother,' Jo reminded him. Not sure she was ready to be presented to the wider circle of family and friends.

'Nonsense. You're part of the family now. Even Taylor's coming tomorrow to be part of the celebrations. Everyone is going to have a great time.' Paul seemed to be trying to convince himself of that.

Jo had heard that his relationship with his eldest was strained. She'd met his stepson, Harry, and stepdaughter, Allegra, but Taylor had been absent from the family home as long as she'd known them. From everything Isabelle had told her, he despised everything his family stood for, so she wondered why he would've agreed to a New Year's Eve party on the private island, and what made him so superior to the rest of the family.

* * *

Whether it was the humidity, or the guilt of leaving her parents behind in snowy England that was keeping her awake, Jo couldn't keep lying in bed staring at the ceiling. She had been afforded every luxury, but she was still restless. Tiptoeing past Isabelle's adjoining room so as not to disturb her, Jo decided to explore the villa a little further.

She'd only seen part of the sprawling property on the way in, but it was enough to intrigue her. Along with the requisite swimming pool and relaxation area, she was sure she'd also seen an open air gym. Not that she was keen to do anything too energetic in this heat, but she was curious as to what other surprises were in store. There was also the matter of her rumbling stomach and her parched throat to attend to. Paul had kept his word and had dinner served to Jo and Isabelle in their rooms, but as delightful as the seafood platter had been, it hadn't quite filled her. The mini fridge provided for them was also in Isabelle's room and she hadn't wanted to disturb her. Yes, this late-night visit was basically a search for the kitchen to find herself a midnight snack…

Padding barefoot along the cool tiled floors, she bypassed the other bedrooms and huge bathrooms, until she came to the large open plan kitchen.

'Wow.' It was about ten times the size of the

box room she'd been living in at her parents' place for the past two years.

She trailed her fingers across the marble countertops and stainless steel appliances. Everything was spotless, and the floor-to-ceiling windows provided a stunning view out to sea. Although it was dark, the glow from the silver moon reflecting on the frothy waves outside was as much light as she needed.

Jo helped herself to a bottle of water from the American-style fridge and carried it over to the window, holding it against her fevered skin as she listened to the soothing sound of the waves. It was all surreal. Usually on Boxing Day she'd still be lying in something of a food hangover from Christmas Day, the remnants of unwrapped presents lying all around the Christmas tree, listening to her father complain about the lack of good programmes on TV. Here, there was no sign Christmas had even happened. It really was a different world. A fantasy land that made her believe she could really leave everything that had happened to her these past two years behind and start again. Maybe she could do so with the money she was being paid to work the holidays.

Not that that was the sole reason she'd agreed to come. Isabelle was a lovely lady and she wanted to be here for her so she could enjoy the celebrations with the rest of the family. Plus, it gave Jo some time away from her parents, and she reckoned they could all do with a break from one another. At least when she was around Isabelle she didn't feel as though she was treading on eggshells, afraid to say the wrong thing and upset her. Regardless of how much still needed to be said.

Things hadn't been right between herself and her parents since she discovered she was adopted upon opening a new bank account. Until then, she hadn't needed, much less seen, her birth certificate, and had ordered a copy of it unaware of the ensuing consequences. Finding out her parents had lied to her her whole life had affected eighteen-year-old Jo deeply, leaving her feeling betrayed and lost. Everything she'd ever known, apparently a lie. She hadn't been ready then to make contact with her biological parents, concentrating on her studies and her nursing career. A part of her not really wanting to accept the truth. After the break-up with Steve, feeling lost, she'd made an attempt to reach out to her birth family. Searching for some sort of stability. Only to find they'd died without her ever getting to know them. It had brought back all of those old feelings of resentment towards her parents, but she'd had to swallow down her pride to ask for their help. In return for lodgings and support she'd suppressed all the questions and anger she'd been holding on to for over a decade for the sake of harmony. The atmosphere at home had been strained ever since, because she blamed them for not letting her discover who she really was.

A few days out of that pressure cooker environment would do wonders for her stress levels.

'Who the hell are you?' The unexpected gruff voice behind her made her jump, and she wasn't proud of the yelp she gave in response either. Clearly she was still wound a little tight.

'J-Jo,' she stuttered as she turned around, responding to the sudden interrogation, regardless of the man's rude manner.

Looking at him attired in a navy tailored suit, she felt extremely underdressed in the moment, aware that she was clad only in her white cotton nightshirt, which wasn't meant to be seen by anyone else, bought only for comfort. She certainly hadn't accounted for it coming under the scrutiny of a handsome, dark-haired stranger who was looking at her as though he could see straight through it. Despite her unease, she resisted her initial urge to try and cover up, and fronted this awkward interaction out. After all, she didn't know who she was speaking to either, and she had as much right to be here as he did. Probably. Unless he was some kind of high-end burglar who'd travelled all this way to rob the Stroud family under the cover of darkness.

'Jo who?' he demanded, but with the few seconds she'd had to recover from the fright, Jo now resented the attitude this stranger was taking with her.

'Who is asking?' she countered, not feeling the need to justify her presence here when she'd been invited, *employed*, by the Strouds to be here.

'Taylor Stroud.' His answer was sufficient to form an O on her lips.

The prodigal son.

'I thought you were arriving tomorrow.'

'I got here early. Again, I'm asking who you are.'

She wondered if he was like this with everyone or if it was evident to him from this brief interaction that she didn't belong, wasn't one of the rich and famous acquaintances who were probably free to come and go as they chose without providing proof of ID.

'Joanna Kirkham. Jo. I've been employed to take care of your grandmother.'

It was hard to see in this limited light, but she was sure he rolled his eyes at her.

'Oh. You're *that* Jo.' The way he said it made it sound as though her reputation had preceded her, and not in a good way. She couldn't for the life of her figure out what she'd done to deserve his obvious disdain. Other than come from a working-class background.

'Yes. I'm her nurse.' For some reason she felt

compelled to add her professional status, though that should have been pretty obvious by now. Her explanation only brought forth a snort of derision.

'Of course you are.'

What the hell was that supposed to mean?

Mr Stroud Jr began to walk towards her, and she backed up against the windowpane as his angular features were highlighted in the moonlight. The high cheekbones and strong jaw would've made him a handsome man if not for the stern look on his face.

'And tell me, Jo, do you often snoop around your clients' houses in the middle of the night?'

It was her turn to frown at the accusation she was doing something untoward. 'You tell me, *Taylor*, do you often hang around in formal attire waiting in the dark to attack strangers?'

'I walked in on you, remember? And you didn't answer my question.'

Jo folded her arms across her chest, her patience and politeness wearing thin. 'No, I don't snoop around anyone's house at night. However, when I'm staying in a very humid room and I don't want to disturb the lady sleeping next door, I will go to the kitchen to get a cold drink. Your family told me to treat the house as my own. I wasn't aware I was under curfew.'

Taylor made a *humph* noise, which suggested he had no comeback to that one.

'Well, I'm a doctor, so I can take care of her from here.'

'Er, Isabelle wants me here, and the family are paying me to look after her. I'm sure you can find something else to do with your time.' She wasn't sure what kind of doctor he was. For all she knew, he'd simply bought the title. The family were certainly rich enough to do whatever they chose. His siblings seemed happy enough to ride the family coattails and didn't feel the need to get in the way of her doing her job. She didn't know what made Taylor so special, or why he appeared to have a problem with her being here.

'I assure you my grandmother's interests are all I have at heart. It's the only reason I came here. I'm not prepared to let anyone take advantage of her.' With that, he tilted his nose in the air, turned on the heel of his expensive leather shoes, and walked away.

'What's that supposed to mean?' she asked into the darkness. The ominous silence that followed his exit told her perhaps this trip away wasn't going to be as relaxing as she'd hoped.

Taylor stomped back to his room and wrenched his tie off before stripping completely and stepping into the shower. The cold water made him take a sharp breath at first, but he soon acclimatised. He needed it to cool off after his unexpected interaction with Jo.

Guilt still ate away at him that he'd been abroad when his beloved grandmother had taken ill and he was only able to see her now, two months on. By the time the news had come through to him she was already recovering at home. He'd video called, and if he'd thought her life was in imminent danger, he would've found a way to get back. However, she'd insisted that he needn't fuss and should concentrate on his work. He'd kept up to date with her recovery, but this was the first chance he'd had to take a break from work.

This mysterious nurse who'd apparently inveigled her way into his grandmother's life in such a short time had already made him wary, and meeting her hadn't done anything to assuage his fears. The family name was a magnet for people who thought they could take advantage and make themselves a few quid. He should know. He'd once thought he'd met the woman of his dreams, someone who was as philanthropic as he hoped to be. But the whole time, she'd been secretly stashing away his money into her own bank account. He wasn't that trusting any more.

Although he still preferred to make use of the family fortune in a more altruistic manner than his father, he was careful about the people he let into his life these days. On this occasion he thought his family should have adopted the same attitude when it came to choosing a companion for his grandmother. From what he could ascertain they knew nothing about this 'Jo', other than the fact that she was capable of doing her job. It wasn't enough for him to entrust his beloved grandmother's welfare to a complete stranger. Con men, and women, were very adept at gaining people's trust. Going under the radar until it was too late and the damage had been done. At least he was able to come out here and provide an objective opinion on this woman and her motives. He could also use the opportunity to provide some medical aid to the locals on neighbouring islands, so this trip hadn't simply been a jolly jaunt added to his carbon footprint.

Taylor needed to know he was doing his best to help others, to remind him he wasn't anything like his father who preferred to sit and count his money than spread the wealth.

As a doctor, he hadn't been able to save everyone who came to him for help, but he could rest easy knowing he'd always done his best. He couldn't say the same about his father.

At thirteen, Taylor had been old enough to remember his father sending him and his mother packing with a hefty cheque, and moving his mistress and her young children into the family home in the same day. It wasn't something easily forgiven. Although he'd still had contact with his father, he'd always felt as though he was something of a nuisance in his father's new life. He'd spent the next couple of years pinballing between two homes, until he found stability at university. He'd no longer felt part of a family. None of what had happened was Harry's, or Allegra's fault, but they weren't close. They had little in common and were very different people. Taylor liked to think he had more of his mother's traits. She was someone who hadn't been too proud to go back to work for a living and was quite happy in her part-time job and living out in the country. His stepfamily seemed to take easily to the good life, and were content to wallow in luxury without a thought for others. It was difficult not to be resentful of the fact that his mother had been treated so appallingly, whilst they'd had everything they'd ever wanted.

Of course, Taylor had enjoyed something of the same pampered lifestyle, but he'd made a vow never to be as callous as his father had been. As soon as he was able to make a difference in other people's lives, he did everything he could to not be just another selfish billionaire only looking out for himself.

He rarely saw any of his family when he was so busy with his work abroad, but he did have a soft spot for his paternal grandmother, Isabelle, who had always been very loving towards him.

She'd made time for him when his father always seemed too busy with work or his new family to bother with him. Her illness had been a shock, and her current circumstances were the reason he was here. His grandmother was still vulnerable, and he knew a thing or two about opportunists taking advantage of kind-natured people.

One thing was for sure, he wasn't going to let this Jo have sole access to his grandmother. He was going to shadow her every move whether she liked it or not.

CHAPTER TWO

'CAN I GET you anything else to eat, Isabelle?' Jo lined up her client's medication on the table for her to take along with a glass of water, eyeing up the buffet-style spread laid out for the guests to help themselves.

'I'm fine. Sit down and eat your breakfast, Jo.'

Jo did as she was told and helped herself to some fresh fruit and yogurt before taking a seat across from Isabelle. Since her late-night encounter with Taylor Stroud, Jo had been unsettled, analysing his every remark. He'd insinuated she was looking after his grandmother for some sinister motive other than simply doing her job. Now she was paranoid the rest of the family would find her lacking in her duties in some way.

'Did you sleep well last night?' She knew sometimes Isabelle's arthritis kept her awake and could provide pain relief if needed.

'Yes, thanks. The fresh air must agree with me. How about you? Did you have a good night's sleep?'

Jo was tempted to tell her about the exchange with her dear grandson, then realised it wouldn't be very professional, and she didn't want to give him any ammunition to use against her.

'The heat made it difficult for me to sleep so I went to the kitchen to get myself some water. I hope that was okay?'

'Of course, dear. Paul told you to make yourself at home.'

She almost asked for that in writing so she could wave it in Taylor's face.

'I might just take some water to bed with me tonight so I don't disturb anyone.'

'Morning.' Taylor arrived as stealthily as he had last night and went to kiss his grandmother on the cheek.

'Taylor! This is a nice surprise. I thought you were supposed to be arriving later today?' Isabelle's eyes lit up at the sight of her grandson and Jo couldn't help but wonder why.

She had to admit he looked good in his light blue linen shirt and cargo shorts. More casual and relaxed than the last time she'd seen him, but no less intimidating as he slid her a dark look.

'I got in last night. I wanted to get a real feel for the place.'

Jo bit her lip.

'I'm so glad you made it.' It was obvious how pleased Isabelle was at him gracing their presence, regardless of the fact that he'd apparently been absent when she'd needed him most.

'I'm so sorry I wasn't there when you were ill. I promise I'll make it up to you.'

'It's fine. I told you to stay where you were, didn't I? You were more use working out there than you could have been to me. Besides, I have Jo now.'

'And me. I brought my medical kit with me. I thought I'd give you a quick examination.' Taylor produced a small bag and proceeded to take out his medical equipment.

It was taking all of Jo's restraint to keep the bubbling anger inside her from manifesting at the end of her fist. 'There's no need, Mr Stroud.'

'Doctor Stroud,' he corrected her with an insincere smile as he placed a blood pressure cuff around Isabelle's arm.

She tried to count to ten in her head so she wouldn't say something in front of her patient that she might come to regret. Unfortunately, she only made it to five. 'As I was saying, *Doctor* Stroud, there's no need for you to trouble yourself. I've already attended to your grandmother's medical needs this morning. Including checking her blood pressure. I'm quite capable of doing my job, thank you.'

'I'm sure you are, but why not make use of a doctor when you have one here?' He put his stethoscope on, presumably so he couldn't hear the rest of her protest, then started pumping up the cuff.

Jo was forced to wait patiently until he'd taken the reading, even though she wanted to scream at him. She didn't know what she'd done to deserve his suspicion, or interference, but she was being severely tested. It took a lot of patience to look after the people she was employed to help. They needed someone to work with them as they recovered from serious illness that left them debilitated. Even Isabelle had needed some time to recover her speech and movement after the stroke. That's why families employed Jo, because she had the skills and patience it took. There was just something about this man that shredded her very last nerve.

Jo folded her arms, foot tapping, waiting until he'd finished his exam. 'Well?'

'Everything seems fine.'

'I told you,' she hissed through gritted teeth.

'It never hurts to get a second opinion now, does it, Jo?'

She didn't appreciate the smug look on his face.

'Good. Now that it's settled that I'm not going to pop my clogs, perhaps I can get on with my day.' It was Isabelle who eventually put an end to the verbal sparring between them. 'Though I need you to do me a favour, Taylor. Could you put those muscles of yours to use and move the mini fridge in my room into Jo's for me? It will be more convenient for her than having to walk all the way to the kitchen.' Isabelle's request apparently took them both by surprise as the look on Taylor's face was probably the same as Jo's. She certainly hadn't asked for it.

'There's no need—'

'Of course. I'll do it later.' Taylor cut off her protest with a promise to carry out his grandmother's wishes at a later time. Hopefully when Jo was nowhere in sight.

'Perhaps we could see about getting her a fan too. I'm not sure the air conditioning is enough,' Isabelle campaigned unnecessarily on her behalf.

'Honestly, there's no need to trouble anyone—'

'I'll speak to Dad and see what we can do. We wouldn't want Ms Kirkham to be uncomfortable.' Although he was playing the role of accommodating host very well, Jo could hear the sneer in his voice.

'Speaking of which, Jo, you must be roasted in that outfit. You don't have to wear it out here. Didn't you bring something more suitable to wear?' Isabelle peered at the blue button-down uniform she had donned to spite Taylor, though she was regretting the non-breathable fabric.

'I thought it would serve as a reminder to everyone that I'm staff. I'm here for you and no other reason.' She directed that at Taylor in case he thought she was here simply for a free holiday.

Isabelle tutted. 'There's no need for that. Yes, you're my nurse, but you're also a friend and a guest. If anyone has a problem with that, they can take it up with me.'

Jo shot Taylor a satisfied smirk and revelled as he cleared his throat, clearly uncomfortable. Good. Now he knew how it felt.

'I thought you might like to go for a walk after breakfast, Grandmother. I could get your chair and take you to the waterfalls if you'd like?' Taylor ignored her and carried on a conversation with his grandmother as though Jo wasn't even in the room.

'That's what I'm here for,' she reminded him.

'As am I. I don't get to spend nearly enough time with my grandmother and I thought this week would be the perfect opportunity.' Taylor gave her a sickly-sweet smile.

'We can all go. It sounds wonderful and how lovely for me to have two medical professionals on hand to tend to my every need.' Isabelle clapped her hands as though she'd come up with the perfect solution. Jo couldn't think of anything worse.

'I'd rather not—'

'I don't think—'

Taylor and Jo stumbled over one another's words in their hurry to get out of the arrangement.

Isabelle set her napkin down on her plate and slowly rose to her feet. 'Jo, you go and get changed into something more suitable for the climate. Taylor, go and have a word with the chef and see if he can prepare us a light picnic to take with us. I'm looking forward to this little outing.'

She was so aglow with excitement at the prospect of getting out and about, neither of her attentive subjects were apparently able to dissuade her from the plan. Jo didn't see that she had any choice but to nod and agree to her client's wishes.

Taylor supposed this little jaunt would give him an opportunity to keep an eye on his grandmother's new best friend, even if he wasn't relishing the thought of spending the day in her company. Certainly they hadn't got off to the best of starts when it appeared Ms Kirkham was the apple of everyone's eye around here. When he'd asked his father what he knew of her this morning he'd described her as 'part of the family'. Something he'd take as an insult if he were her. In his eyes, the Stroud family hadn't done anything to be proud of. At least not with the fortune and possibilities at their disposal.

He did his best to share the wealth and provide aid to the less fortunate. Not that it meant much to his father, or his step-siblings who thought that his job was a pet project like their whims into starting their own clothes labels or interior design. Various fields in which they had no experience or qualifications, merely an interest at the time. He wasn't sure they understood how much training he'd had to be where he was, or if they cared. At least his mother was proud of him, even if he didn't see her as often as he should. Work kept them both busy, but they kept in touch.

The only time he'd felt accepted by his father was when he'd been with Imogen. She seemed to blend in seamlessly with his stepfamily. Now he knew why. She'd apparently been as motivated by money as they were. Once they'd split up he was back to being the pariah of the family. Almost as if they blamed him for taking her away from them. As though it was his fault she'd had to resort to lying and stealing money from him. He'd been left feeling, again, that he hadn't been good enough to be loved. Just as he'd felt when his father took on a new family. He'd since given up trying to gain their approval and was happier on his travels, alone.

When it came to his father's new family, he couldn't get over the feeling that they could do so much more if they weren't so concerned with themselves and that constant desire to add to their bank balance. Goodness knew why when they already had enough money to last them a lifetime.

'Do you have a parasol to keep the sun off

you?' he asked his grandmother as he met her on the veranda.

She scowled at him. 'I'm not some fragile Edwardian noblewoman who'll faint at the first glimpse of the sun. Jo made sure I have sun cream on, and I have a hat.'

She plonked a large-brimmed straw hat on her head as she got into her wheelchair, not looking her chipper self. He wished he'd been a fly on the wall when Jo had displayed similar concerns, sure she wouldn't have received any better reception than he just had. It gave him some satisfaction to think of his grandmother putting up something of a fight against Jo as she'd attempted to administer some protection against the sun. Perhaps his grandmother wasn't as vulnerable as he'd imagined, though he only had her best interests at heart.

'We just don't want you getting burnt, or suffering from heat stroke. We're both trying to take care of you, Isabelle.' Jo appeared then and he was chastened by her words. It was true, they were both simply making sure she was safe and he shouldn't have taken any pleasure in the idea of his grandmother resisting attempts to help her. Although he still had his suspicions about Jo, perhaps for one afternoon, he could set them aside so they could enjoy a walk.

'I'm not a child,' his grandmother huffed, letting them know her fighting spirit was still going strong. Something he was grateful for when her health hadn't been the best.

Taylor had worried about her since the stroke, but he was more afraid now that in his absence he'd let a snake into the nest. The one thing he could do was let it be known that he wasn't going to stand for any kind of manipulation of a vulnerable person.

'We know you're not, Isabelle, but as you said, you have two medical professionals by your side. We would be lacking in our duties if we let anything happen to you.' Jo soothed their patient with some common sense and soft-soaping.

Sufficient that Taylor's grandmother stopped grumbling. About appropriate attire for the weather at least.

'Well let's get on with it, or it'll be dark by the time we get moving.'

'Yes, Grandmother,' he said with a sigh, happening to catch Jo's eye. She gave him a half-smile and for a moment they appeared to bond, before she looked away again.

They both reached for the handles of the wheelchair at the same time.

'I've got it.'

'She's my grandmother.'

'Now, now, there's no need to fight over me.

Taylor, dear, you push me, and Jo can walk along-side me. She's a much prettier view.'

Taylor had to agree with his grandmother as he took control. Jo walked ahead, following the path he assumed his father had made down to the waterfall. It was a wonder he hadn't had the whole thing tarmacked, or built a bridge to the mainland to make life easier for himself. He wasn't senti-mental about destroying natural beauty.

Speaking of which, *Jo looks lovely today.*

'Pardon?' She turned around and he realised with horror that he'd voiced that out loud.

'I was just remarking on how much better you look out of your uniform. I mean, in your casual clothes.' He stumbled over his excuses, somewhat taken aback by his response to the sight of her today.

His journey to the island had been fraught with delays and hot, cramped conditions, and as a re-sult his mood had been...irascible. He hadn't been able to see her clearly in the dark, and his mind had been elsewhere. Now, however, with the sun-light shining through her white shirt dress, which showed off her curvy figure and toned legs, he could see she was as beautiful as the local scen-ery. Even her clear green eyes seemed to be spar-kling like the tropical waters surrounding the island. She looked at home here.

'Well, I didn't want you to think I was forgetting my place here.' She narrowed those beautiful eyes at him and he felt himself flush with shame at his behaviour last night. He didn't like to be judged himself, either by his own family or outsiders, and it hadn't been fair of him to make assumptions about her. It didn't mean he wasn't wary about her motives for getting close to his grandmother and the rest of the family, but he wouldn't find anything out by being hostile.

'Sorry about last night. It had been a bit of an arduous journey for me to get here. I shouldn't have taken it out on you.' Taylor heaved the backpack containing their refreshments further up onto his back.

'It's fine.' Jo sighed. 'Let's just enjoy the day. Can I carry that for you? I want to do something useful. I'm still on the clock after all.'

Her tongue-and-cheek comment along with her offer to help went some way to thawing relations between them as Taylor handed over the bag.

Isabelle glanced between them both. 'Is there something going on between you that I don't know about?'

Taylor didn't want to upset her by admitting his suspicions, or embarrass himself by getting a telling off from his grandmother who wouldn't hear a bad thing said about her nurse. So he decided not to mention his late night altercation with Jo, and hoped she would do the same.

'Not at all. We're just getting to know one another. Aren't we, Taylor?' Jo fixed the backpack around her shoulders and batted her eyelashes at him, apparently on board with this truce. For now.

'One big happy family.' He grinned, navigating the wheelchair down the lane towards the vast green landscape ahead.

'What about your family, Jo? Do they mind that you're not home for Christmas?' Isabelle said.

Taylor didn't miss Jo's brief scowl at his grandmother's questions. He wondered what the background story was, and if they had more in common than he'd first thought. Perhaps she didn't get along with her family either.

'It's just Mum and Dad at home. I'm sure they're glad I'm out from under their feet for a while.'

'Oh? You still live at home?' Taylor's curiosity piqued at this new information. He would have had Jo pegged for an independent woman who valued her personal space. Certainly he hadn't been able to move out of home quick enough to stay in student digs as soon as he'd been old enough. A life of luxury wasn't everything if you had a social conscience too. He'd wanted to go out on his own and make a difference in the world. As well as getting some space from those who didn't understand him, and vice versa. It was ironic that he'd ended up adding more money to the family pot with his innovative medical invention—a portable device able to test bloods on site for all manner of ailments and send the information to the nearest hospital via satellite phone. A lifesaver in some of the remote areas he worked in. Money-making had never been his objective, only a need to improve a service for his patients.

Jo plucked a long blade of grass from along the side of the laneway and folded it between her fingers. 'At the moment. I'm hoping to get another place of my own this year.'

It was a carefully worded comment that prompted so many more questions. Why did she have to move back in with her parents if she'd previously lived in her own place? Did she live with someone else? Had there been a break-up? He hadn't seen a wedding ring on her finger, but he knew from bitter experience that any failed relationship was painful to deal with. Of course, her private life wasn't any of his business. Unless it had any bearing on her role here. He was sure his father had done some background checks before employing her as a carer for his mother, and he was sure she was capable of doing her job, but he was concerned that she might be using it to get close enough to take advantage of his grandmother.

'I'm sure they're missing you. What do you usually do at Christmas?' Taylor's grandmother appeared oblivious to Jo's caginess, probing deeper into her personal circumstances. He listened on with fascination. His questions could wait for another date. Presumably when he'd done a little bit more research and had information he might be able to confront her with. Perhaps she had nothing to hide and he was simply projecting his past painful experience onto someone who wanted nothing more than to help an elderly lady, but that instinct he'd developed since his break-up for smelling trouble was on high alert.

'We just have a quiet one. I didn't miss anything, I'm sure.'

'New Year's out here is going to be entirely different. My son doesn't do understated, or quiet. He has quite the party planned.'

'So I hear. I'm looking forward to the celebrations.' Jo swung around again, her blond ponytail swishing as she abruptly ended the conversation and began marching ahead.

Yup. She was definitely hiding something, and Taylor was determined to find out what.

The view was stunning. As they made their way into the clearing, Jo could only stand and stare in awe. The sound of the thundering waterfall was deafening, but welcome. Hopefully drowning out any more questions about her home life. Although Isabelle had been sympathetic to her plight, she didn't want to have to confess about the break-up of her relationship and subsequent financial difficulties to Taylor. It was embarrassing enough that she'd been left destitute without having to recount the details leading up to it to someone who probably didn't have any concept of what it meant.

Taylor had been born into money, and by all accounts, made more of it every time he breathed. She wasn't jealous, she just wished her own circumstances were different. Enough that she could live a quiet life without the constant worry about how she was going to survive, or what the future held. Issues she was certain someone like Taylor would never have to deal with. Good for him.

'There's a little shady spot here. Why don't we stop for a moment?' Taylor was still able to make his voice heard above the roar of water spilling down the rock face, and Jo was keen to have a little break too. With the weight of the bag on her back, and the heat of the sun shining down, she was beginning to flag.

'Good idea.' She dropped the bag where she stood and unpacked the blanket Taylor had put in for them to sit on. He spread it on the ground and held out a hand to his grandmother to help her out of the chair.

'I think I'll just stay where I am, thanks, in case I can't get up again. You and Jo sit down. You've been doing all the heavy work.' Isabelle, either oblivious to the friction between her companions, or choosing to ignore it, was forcing them to sit down together in enforced harmony.

Jo perched on the farthest piece of the tartan blanket that she could, but it made no difference when Taylor joined her, his body and long legs dominating the space. So much so that his thighs were touching hers, and she could feel his body heat through the thin fabric of her dress. Despite being out of the direct sun, her skin became feverish. It was the closest she'd been to a man since the break-up. That was the only reason she was responding the way she was. It had absolutely nothing to do with the muscular thigh pressed intimately against her outer leg.

'Jo?'

'Hmm?'

'I was just asking if you'd like a drink?' Taylor was looking at her with amusement and she realised she'd been so caught up in her body's physical reaction to him, and what it meant, that she hadn't heard the question.

'Sorry. I was miles away. Yes, I'd love a drink of lemonade. Thank you.' At this point it didn't matter. She just needed something to cool down the heat of her embarrassment. The last thing she needed was to find herself attracted to an arrogant billionaire who clearly despised her. Actually, worse than that was the thought that he might be able to tell.

Taylor poured them all a drink and she busied herself laying out the spread the kitchen had provided for their little outing. Lots of fresh fruit and dainty sandwiches for them to snack on. She plated up some food for Isabelle before tucking in herself.

'It's lovely down here, isn't it? The young ones like to swim in the pool there.'

'It looks refreshing,' Jo agreed, following Isabelle's wistful gaze down to the clear pool at the foot of the waterfalls.

'I might go in for a dip.' Taylor got to his feet, kicking off his footwear and unbuttoning his shirt.

Jo swallowed, trying not to stare, even though curiosity as to what was beneath that shirt was getting the better of her.

'You go too,' Isabelle urged her.

'I couldn't possibly…' Jo spluttered, uncomfortable with the idea of stripping off down to her bikini to frolic in the water with Taylor. She had only put it on under her dress in case she got the opportunity to do a little sun worshipping, in private. Who wouldn't come out here and hope to go back to wintry England without a tan?

'Ah, come on. We can keep an eye on Gran

from down there.' Taylor whipped off his shirt, baring his smooth, delineated torso.

Jo took a sip of lemonade to quench her sudden thirst.

'I'm just going to close my eyes for a few minutes so you may as well go and enjoy yourself.' Isabelle handed Jo her empty plate and settled back into her wheelchair for a nap.

Jo didn't know what defence she had left, save for saying she didn't want to cavort half naked with Taylor in the water for the sake of her peace of mind. She didn't want to lust over someone who'd made her a candidate for anger management classes within five minutes of meeting him.

'I'll maybe just go and dip my toes in. That way I'll be able to race back if you need me.'

Eyes closed, Isabelle simply mumbled her agreement as her grandson tore on down towards the water. He was like a different person today. Carefree. Fun. Accommodating. Even at breakfast there had still been an atmosphere between them, almost resentment about her presence here. Now, however, he was acting as though they were besties. Perhaps that's exactly what it was, an 'act' for his grandmother's benefit. A truce they'd silently agreed to so as not to upset her, but which was now causing Jo anxiety. Because she didn't want to like him. Her life was messy enough without the added complication of a crush on her employer's son.

Even if she ever got over the pain of her ex's betrayal, Taylor was probably the worst person to set her sights on. All those close to her seemed to let her down and she'd learned the hard way that the only person she could trust was herself. She was even having doubts about that now...

Jo carefully picked her way through the foliage in her now bare feet, casting a glance back every now and then to make sure Isabelle was all right. The spray drifting on the breeze from the waterfall was cooling on her skin, and the tall trees and giant palm leaves were providing shade. It was paradise.

Whilst Taylor had headed up to a greater height, she walked down towards the water's edge in the shallows to paddle her feet.

With a Tarzan-like call, Taylor leapt off the ledge and landed with a splash in the pool, causing a shower to soak Jo in the process. The sudden cold made her gasp as she fought for breath.

'Sorry,' Taylor called to her as he emerged from the clear water, washing his hands over his face and hair. Though the grin on his face showed no sign of apology at all.

Jo looked down at her dress, which was practically see-through anyway now. She looked at Taylor who walloped both hands down on the surface of the water and caused another soaking. His smile growing wider by the second.

'Oh, you're asking for it—' A need for revenge overriding common sense and self-preservation, Jo whipped off her dress and waded into the water in her bright yellow bikini.

Taylor didn't move. Challenging her to do her worst. With a determined stride, she made her way towards him until he was within reaching distance. Two hands in front of her, she pushed a wall of water at him, then swam away laughing as he shook his head from side to side like a wet dog after the resulting tsunami. Revenge was so very sweet. And wet.

Before he could retaliate, she ducked in behind the waterfall into a secret rocky grotto. Taylor quickly followed, breaching the curtain of water to join her. Okay, so her hiding place wasn't so secret after all.

'Believe it or not this is the first time I've been here,' he told her, coming to stand near her, water dripping down his muscular chest.

'The waterfall?' It was hard to concentrate when they were so close, seemingly locked away from the rest of the world, and she was increasingly aware of her own state of undress. Especially when his gaze flicked appreciatively over her body. Jo crossed her arms over her chest, feeling her nipples harden in the cool air.

Taylor sank back down into the water and broke the intimacy of the moment that seemed to be happening between them. 'Er, no. I mean the island.'

'But your family own it.' She couldn't believe that he wouldn't take advantage of exclusive access to this place any time he wanted. Given the chance, she was sure she could happily spend the rest of her days here. Especially if she had a full staff of people on hand taking care of her every need.

He shrugged. 'My father owns it. He owns a lot of things. It doesn't mean I want to be part of the whole show.'

Jo raised an eyebrow. 'But you are. Aren't you part of the empire? Why wouldn't you enjoy the benefits that come with that?'

He was such a complex character. Someone who appeared to have the world at his feet, but resented it at the same time. His stepbrother and stepsister didn't seem to have a problem with it, embracing the life of luxury and privilege the family name afforded them. Jo didn't recall ever hearing about their careers outside of Stroud Technologies. It was obvious that there was a story behind Taylor's reluctance to be part of the family, and a reason why he was choosing now to make an effort with them.

The frown was back, transforming his otherwise handsome face into that surly man she'd met last night in the dark. Then he sighed and relaxed again. 'Trust me, it's conflicting for me too. I think the money my family has is obscene, yet it enables me to help out disadvantaged communities I probably wouldn't be able to reach otherwise.'

'But you're a doctor. I'm sure that would've happened anyway.' Whilst she admired the fact that he'd carved out his own career, she didn't see what the conflict was with his family's status. He could choose to walk away from it altogether if he felt so strongly, be financially independent. Something she hoped to be again someday.

'Not to the same extent. I run free clinics abroad when I can.'

'Is that why you decided to come out here?'

'Partly,' he said ominously. 'Anyway, enough about me. We should probably get back.'

Taylor made a move first and she followed. Except she slipped on a rock underfoot and went under the water, spluttering as the water went up her nose and down her throat, making it difficult to breathe. Then, as she was beginning to panic, two large hands were at her waist, lifting her up out of the water.

'Are you okay?'

After she was done coughing and wiping the water from her eyes, she could see Taylor staring at her, concern etched on his face. He was standing close, holding her by the arms.

'I'm fine, thank you. I just lost my footing and swallowed some water.'

'Just take some deep breaths,' he said, holding her whilst she did so.

She would have been embarrassed if it wasn't for the other emotions and sensations currently flooding her body. The awareness of his touch upon her, his genuine concern and kindness towards her—all things that had been missing from her life for so long—awakened something else inside her. Desire.

'You're shaking. It must be the shock.'

Before Jo had a chance to protest, Taylor had swept her up into his arms and was treading water, carrying her back to dry land. She had no choice but to wrap her arms around his neck for support, creating further skin to skin contact. The steady beat of his heart as she pressed against his chest was as reassuring as his body heat.

'You can put me down now,' she tried to insist once they were out of the water, but Taylor was undeterred, carrying her back to the picnic spot.

'What on earth has happened?' Isabelle was visibly distressed at the sight, and Jo could've kicked herself as well as Taylor for worrying her unnecessarily.

'Nothing. I had a little fall. Taylor is overreacting.' She narrowed her eyes at him, trying to get him to set her down when she was extremely aware there wasn't very much keeping their naked bodies apart.

'As a medical professional too, I'm sure you would do the same.' The mood had changed between them again as he teased her. She supposed it should be easier than the sexual tension she didn't know how to deal with, but she didn't like him to think he had the upper hand. Life had taught her never to give control away, and at present, she was very much at his mercy.

'Hmm, not sure I have the upper body strength. I would've had to drag you up here by the ankles instead.' She pried herself away from his bare chest and made an attempt to stand on her own.

'Thank goodness we didn't have to do that then.' He dumped her unceremoniously onto the blanket and wrapped it around her until she was swaddled like a newborn, and virtually unable to move.

'This really isn't necessary,' she spat. He was enjoying her discomfort way too much.

'I'll go and get our clothes. You stay here and dry off.'

She didn't have much choice, but she was grateful that he'd at least covered her up. Once they had their clothes back on perhaps she wouldn't feel so vulnerable and out of her comfort zone.

* * *

Taylor let out a shaky breath as he jogged away, needing some space. And a cold shower. The pool at the waterfall would have to do. Carrying a wet, half-naked Jo in his arms had seemed like a good idea at the time, but he'd been left feeling decidedly…uncomfortable. It was natural to be attracted to the blonde beauty, but that didn't mean he had to act on it. If only his body would take that on board.

He'd tried to downplay the moment he'd chosen the worst possible time to respond to her as a hot-blooded man, rather than a suspicious bystander, by teasing her. At least it had put her off the scent that he was attracted to her, even if it was liable to make things between them frosty again. That was probably preferable in the circumstances.

He dived back into the cool water, momentarily cleansing himself of his sin. It wouldn't do to have inappropriate thoughts about the woman he'd come here to investigate. Perhaps if it hadn't been for his past experiences, he would never have thought to be suspicious of his grandmother's nurse. However, his ex had got close to the family too, only to siphon away a great deal of his money whilst he'd been deceived by her charms. It wasn't the money that bothered him, it was the betrayal, the lies and deceit, which had been more difficult to move past. He didn't wish for his grandmother to be hurt the way he'd been if Jo had similar intentions.

In his case, it had been a beautiful woman who'd convinced him she was as dedicated to helping others as he was, who'd used his generosity for her own benefit. Soliciting handouts for alleged charitable acts she'd claimed to be carrying out. Something he'd never thought to check on. He'd believed he was helping to establish a new venture abroad providing medical care for disadvantaged people, because she'd told him all of her great plans in detail, and he'd never thought to question her legitimacy. A mistake that had cost him dearly, and not just in a financial sense. That broken trust was something he didn't think could ever be repaired, and the reason he couldn't take Jo at face value.

Appearances could be deceptive, and he wasn't sure his grandmother would recover if she experienced such a brutal betrayal. He certainly hadn't.

It was inconvenient to say the least to find his body had apparently forgotten to be as wary as the rest of him when it came to beautiful women.

Once Taylor had recovered his composure, and was sure he wouldn't embarrass either of them, he did one last lap and climbed out of the pool. His sodden shorts wouldn't leave anything to the imagination if he couldn't control his impulses, so he hoped they'd dry quickly once he was out in the sun again.

Taylor stopped to grab Jo's dress from the nearby rocks, still damp from his horsing around earlier. It was a reminder that he'd started the nonsense, and any resulting moments of intimacy had been entirely his own fault. He'd let his guard down so much with her he'd almost shared some very personal information and private thoughts about his relationship with his family. Along with the reasons he was out here. That hadn't been part of the plan, but it was easy to see why the rest of the family had been so beguiled by her. He would have to stay alert around her for the duration of his stay on the island.

By the time he reached the others, Jo had already packed their things away, and was standing waiting in that sunny two-piece bikini. He tossed her dress over but didn't miss the way her eyes lingered on his body as he put his shirt back on.

'Could we walk on down to the beach? I'd like to feel the sea air on my face for a while.' His grandmother's request was surprising on top of the outing they'd just undertaken, considering she'd appeared to doze off whilst they'd been at the pool.

'Wouldn't you like to go back and rest for a while, Isabelle?'

'Jo's right. We wouldn't want you to overdo it.'

He'd been hoping they'd all be going their separate ways, giving him some space from Jo to remember exactly why he was here.

'I've been sitting here whilst you two were playing in the water. Now it's my turn.' Taylor's grandmother folded her hands in her lap and tilted her chin up into the air, letting them both know there would be no further argument.

He and Jo took up their positions and made the trip to the shore, even though it meant doubling back on themselves. Of course, despite his best intentions, he couldn't fail to notice that Jo's dress was clinging intimately to her curves, and he prayed for the torture to end.

CHAPTER THREE

ISABELLE SEEMED DETERMINED to get her own way today, regardless of whatever cost to Jo's peace of mind. She was used to her client's strong will, and was usually a fan. After all, that's what had helped her recovery so far. That stubborn determination had driven her to recover most of the use in her left-hand side again, which had been partially paralysed after the stroke. Isabelle, despite her frailty, had worked with a physiotherapist to regain her strength and thankfully, much of her mobility. However, in the circumstances, Jo longed for some compliance so she could retreat to her own quarters.

Which didn't include a view of Taylor's wet shorts cupping his backside. It was her own fault for falling so behind, but she'd been attempting to avoid small talk with him. Or worse, the easy repartee they seemed to have fallen into. When they got too comfortable with one another she apparently forgot about the man who'd 'greeted' her in the dark last night. And that was the version of Taylor Stroud she needed to cling to if she was to go home from this trip unscathed.

'Isn't that glorious?' Isabelle's words didn't do the sight justice when Jo finally saw it for herself.

Of course she'd seen the stunning vista on her arrival to the island, but actually being on the beach looking out at the Pacific Ocean was something else. Whilst Taylor pushed his grandmother down the wooden walkway, Jo pulled off her sandals and walked on the fine golden sand, revelling in the feel of it beneath her feet. If she ignored the development the Strouds had made nearby to make it their home, she could almost imagine she'd been cast away on a desert island. With the palm trees providing shade and already having found fresh water, she wondered if she could've survived here without the chef and kitchen staff back at the house. The soothing sound of the waves breaking on the shore made all of her problems seem so far away she wished she could stay here for ever.

'Yet everyone else is sitting up by the pool.' Taylor sighed, and Jo understood his frustration, yet was selfishly glad they were the only ones here.

It would've been spoiled by pampered guests stretched out with cocktails in their hands, video calling their friends and live blogging instead of living in the moment.

'They'll come down later for drinks. There are daybeds and a beach bar further on up,' Isabelle said.

'Of course there are,' Taylor darkly responded to his grandmother's new information.

'Well, I like it here.' Jo dumped the bag on the sand and stretched.

'I'd like to take a walk down to the sea.' Isabelle bent down to take off her shoes, clearly feeling the need to experience the sand between her toes too.

Jo and Taylor both rushed to assist her, each taking an arm to help her up out of the wheelchair.

'None of your shenanigans this time. I've just about dried out,' Jo warned Taylor as they made their way down to the water, arm in arm with the elderly woman.

He simply grinned in response, as if to say he wasn't making any promises. Though Jo didn't imagine he would do anything to upset his grandmother. They clearly doted on one another, even though they hadn't seen much of each other in the time she'd been working for the family. It made her wonder why he kept his distance, and why he was back on the scene now. He'd made his distaste over his family's wealth clear, so it didn't make any sense why he'd choose to come to the island that was the ultimate display of grandstanding.

'I can't remember the last time I did this.' Isabelle lit up like a child seeing the ocean for the first time. Jo was glad they could do something nice for her after the trouble she'd had with her health lately. It was the reason she'd been employed by the Strouds, to care for her through her recovery, but seeing a patient back on their feet wasn't always part of Jo's experience. Often when she was involved with an elderly patient it was towards the end of their lives and they weren't as mobile as Isabelle was.

'I can manage on my own now,' she insisted, paddling out into the sea.

Jo and Taylor let go of her and watched on like two anxious parents.

'Don't go out too far,' she called, but Isabelle simply waved her away.

'She's a stubborn so-and-so,' Taylor laughed.

'It must run in the family.'

'Don't knock it. It's what makes us survivors.' A strange expression crossed Taylor's face, then disappeared as quickly as it appeared.

The Stroud family didn't strike Jo as 'survivors', rather entrepreneurs who'd been fortunate compared to most people. Though she agreed with the sentiment. It was sheer pigheadedness that had got her through her troubles. A determination that she wouldn't let her ex ruin her life. Something she was still working through. Taylor was giving all the signs of someone who'd gone through a similar rough time, even if it wasn't a severe lack of money that could possibly have caused him problems.

'I hear you,' she muttered, drawing an inquisitive glance from Taylor.

Suddenly, Isabelle let out a yelp and toppled back into the water. Jo didn't think twice about running to her, with Taylor alongside.

'Isabelle?' She was lying flat on her back, her face contorted in pain.

'I… I think something…stung me.' Her breathing was shallow, her words slurring.

'We need to get her out of the water.' Taylor grabbed hold of his grandmother under one arm, and Jo got the other so they could pull her out onto the sand. Her heart was racing, but her nursing instincts took over from the fear and anxiety surrounding the situation.

'There's something moving in the water…' Jo pointed at a strange, spiky looking fish nearby as Taylor checked the wound site.

'I thought it was just a rock…' Isabelle's voice was starting to sound distant, as though she was drifting into unconsciousness. Whatever happened, Jo knew she had a better chance of survival if they kept her awake.

'Stay with us, Isabelle. Can you tell me how you're feeling?'

'Hot… I feel sick…'

'It could be a stonefish. I did a bit of reading

up about the local wildlife before I came out.' Jo knew that particular species could be deadly and had to be acted upon immediately.

'There's a puncture site on her foot—barbs of some sort still in it,' Taylor surmised.

Jo felt Isabelle's forehead. 'She's burning up.'

'Her blood pressure's dropping, heartbeat irregular, and the entire leg is beginning to swell already. That's the venom in her blood stream. We need to get those barbs out.' The pain on Taylor's face as he lifted her bleeding, discoloured foot suggested he blamed himself for somehow failing his grandmother. Jo recognised it because she felt the same way.

Then she realised Isabelle had stopped breathing and her nursing instincts well and truly kicked in. 'Taylor, she's not breathing. I'm starting CPR.'

Jo couldn't stop to see how he took the news. Instead, she tilted Isabelle's head back and made sure her airways were clear before starting to deliver chest compressions.

Cardiac arrest meant the heart was no longer pumping blood around the body, preventing oxygen to the brain. If Jo didn't make any attempt to keep the blood and oxygen circulating herself, Isabelle would die in minutes.

Kneeling in the sand, the water lapping around her, Jo began CPR. With the heel of one hand in the centre of Isabelle's chest, she placed her other hand on top and interlocked her fingers. Arms straight, she pushed down hard in a desperate hope to revive Isabelle. 'One, two, three—'

Carefully, Taylor pulled out the small barbs from Isabelle's foot and set them aside, sweat forming on his forehead with the sustained effort he was putting in to try and save his grandmother's life.

'How the hell are we going to get an ambulance out here?' Despite all of their efforts, Jo knew it could be in vain if they didn't get Isabelle to hospital for proper treatment. She was beginning to tire, and goodness knew she couldn't keep this up until someone happened to stumble across them.

'Let me take over, Jo,' Taylor pleaded, apparently sensing her struggle.

'I can manage.' She didn't want him to think she wasn't capable when this was the very reason she'd been employed to look after his grandmother.

'Please. I need to do something useful.' It was a plea she couldn't ignore when he looked so anguished. Jo could relate to that feeling of helplessness. That's exactly how she'd felt for two years after what her ex had done, trying to wrestle control of circumstances that had been taken out of her hands. At least here she could relieve one person of that feeling, if only for a moment.

'Okay.' She relinquished control, for both his

and Isabelle's sakes as her arms were beginning to feel the strain.

Taylor came to her side and they quickly switched positions.

'My phone's in the bag. Phone my dad and tell him what's happened. We need a helicopter, plane, anything to get her to the nearest hospital. We can't wait for help to come to us.' Taylor carried on, arms outstretched, fingers linked, pushing down on his frail grandmother's chest. It seemed Taylor's doctor side had come to the fore too, even though this was his loved one lying unresponsive.

Jo emptied the contents of the bag onto the sand until she spotted his phone. He shouted out his password so she could access his contacts and phone his father. She tried not to panic him as she relayed what had happened, told him their whereabouts and left the rest up to him. All the while she was watching Taylor work, and praying for a miracle. This wasn't what any of them had imagined when they'd flown out here for New Year's celebrations.

'Look in that bag and see if there's any hot water to soak the wound. It's the best temperature to treat this kind of injury.'

Jo followed Taylor's instruction and located the flask of hot water Isabelle had no doubt requested for her afternoon tea. Not wanting to cause any further injury, she tried a little of the steaming liquid onto her hand to make sure it was bearable before pouring it onto the wound.

Jo marvelled at his extensive knowledge and wondered how often he treated this kind of injury. It was certainly something she'd never had to deal with before and wasn't ashamed to admit she was a little out of her depth.

'Listen! I think I heard her take a breath.' Taylor stopped chest compressions and bent down to listen to Isabelle's chest, and checked her wrist for a pulse.

Jo held her breath until he confirmed it.

'She's breathing.'

'Isabelle? Can you hear me? It's Jo. We need you to try and stay awake for us, okay?' Jo did her best to reassure her as she came to on the sand with her and Taylor leaning over her.

Isabelle was shaking and mumbling incoherently now, and they moved quickly to get her into the recovery position. Now that the immediate danger appeared to have passed, the shock and disbelief at what had happened seemed to set in. She found herself suddenly teary, but the only thing more surprising than that was Taylor reaching out to give her hand a squeeze. Perhaps a silent signal to let her know he was feeling equally emotional, but also a reminder that he was here with her. A touching gesture she would never have expected from someone who'd made no attempt to hide the fact he resented her very presence so far.

It was possible there was a thaw setting in, hopefully due to the fact he was finally realising they were both here for Isabelle's benefit.

The moment was soon interrupted by a cacophony of noise and chaos as the family came running down onto the beach crying and yelling, followed by the arrival of a helicopter further up. Taylor covered his grandmother with his body, protecting her from the sand and debris whipped up.

They weren't ideal conditions for a patient transport with no paramedics or stretchers, but between them they managed to get Isabelle on board. Jo made a move to get in alongside her, but that idea was shot down by Taylor.

'I'll go with her in case anything happens. I'll phone ahead to the hospital and let them know we're coming.'

'Okay. You're the doctor,' Jo conceded and backed off. It was his grandmother and he was the senior medical professional here. It was his call.

Nobody should be relying on her judgement these days. She was someone who apparently hadn't known who she'd got into bed and business with despite spending every minute of every day with Steve. As a result, she questioned everything she did lately. Letting her patient walk into unknown waters and almost die as a result was simply another example of her bad decision-making. It was no wonder Taylor had trouble trusting her. He clearly had better judgement than she could ever hope for.

'Thanks, Jo. For everything.' Out of the blue, Taylor offered her his gratitude, along with a half-smile. She supposed it was his way of apologising for the way he'd treated her up until now, as well as recognition that she'd been partly responsible for saving his grandmother's life.

Hopefully he'd remember that the next time their paths crossed.

As the helicopter rose up into the sky she knew Isabelle was in the best hands, and hoped for a positive outcome. However, she couldn't shake off the notion that she'd let Isabelle and her family down. She'd been distracted today, her thoughts straying to Isabelle's grandson instead of the real reason she was out here, and if she couldn't do her job then she was no use to anyone.

Taylor let himself into the villa, doing his best not to alert anyone to his presence. He wanted some downtime before he faced the family. Even though he'd already spoken to his father and reassured everyone that his grandmother was going to be fine, he knew he'd be bombarded with a hundred and one questions. After a long day he wasn't ready for that just yet.

He was just thankful that he and Jo had been there. Though he had experience of working in exotic climes, it was Jo who'd spotted the stonefish and saved precious time, which might otherwise have been wasted trying to find out what had happened. As scary as the whole situation had been, at least they'd been able to move swiftly to help his grandmother and he was grateful for Jo's calming influence as well as her medical expertise.

As he'd waited at the hospital for news, he'd had time to reflect on everything that had happened on the island since his arrival. It was possible, he supposed, that he'd got Jo all wrong. Certainly, she'd been as concerned as he for his grandmother's welfare and had done everything in her power to save her. She'd even been a little emotional by the end of it all. He should probably give her a break, stop giving her a hard time and let her get on with the job she'd come here to do. At least once his grandmother had recovered and was back on the island with them, or they both went back to England.

The hospital had treated his grandmother with antivenom, given oxygen and fluids upon arrival. If she'd been stung elsewhere, or he and Jo hadn't acted so quickly, she might not have survived.

Something he didn't want to share with his family. If there weren't any complications, she should be back with them in a day or two, so he didn't see the point in upsetting anyone unnecessarily.

He went to his room to change out of the clothes he'd been wearing all day into some more comfortable jogging bottoms and T-shirt. Fooling around with Jo at the pool seemed like a lifetime ago now after spending most of the afternoon and evening in the tiny hospital on one of the bigger neighbouring islands. It was clear they were struggling with the ratio of staff to patients, and he'd even had to volunteer his services to help out so he could get his grandmother the treatment she needed. At least it gave him validation about this whole trip being more than sussing out Jo's motivations. It was obvious they needed extra funding out here, and in the meantime he'd set up an emergency clinic of his own nearby. For now, he needed something to eat and drink, and a moment to collect his thoughts.

He made his way to the kitchen and flicked the light on. Only to find Jo sitting at the breakfast bar, jacket on and suitcase at her feet.

'What are you doing?'

'I, er, I'm…what's happening to Isabelle? Your father said she's recovering well.' She deftly changed the subject, but Taylor wasn't going to walk away without an explanation.

'She is. All her test results were fine, but they're

going to keep her in for a couple of days just to make sure there are no complications or after-effects. Now, what are you doing?' This had all the hallmarks of their first meeting. Although this time around he was more irritated by the thought of her leaving than her presence. A development he'd never expected and wasn't sure how to deal with.

'I'm glad she's going to be okay. I let her down.'

'How did you work that one out? We were both there at her command, got her medical treatment and saved her life.'

'I think you did most of that, but that's not the point. If I'd done my job properly, we wouldn't have even been there. She'd done too much, been in the sun too long—'

'And none of that had anything to do with what happened. You don't need to play the martyr, Jo. It was an accident no one could have foreseen.'

'Which might never have happened if I'd been vigilant.' Jo seemed determined to beat herself up over what had happened, and whilst it was always unnerving when a loved one was involved in a medical emergency, this hadn't been anyone's fault. Taylor didn't understand why she was doubting herself when she'd done everything that could possibly have been expected of her and more.

'So, what, you're going to fly back home?'

'I hadn't figured that bit out yet. It's not as easy as booking a flight online. I was sitting here thinking about what I was going to say to your father so he'd help me out.'

'Do you always run away when things don't go your way? That's not very reassuring for your patients, is it?' He knew he was being facetious, but he wanted her to see how ridiculous she was being. Even if that meant riling her up in the process.

'I'm not running away. I've never run away from anything in my life. But I was paid to do a job here and since your grandmother is in hospital there's no need for me to stay, is there?'

Taylor didn't doubt for one second that Jo was the sort of person who would always face a challenge head on, which made her apparent decision to flee all the more mind-boggling.

'As far as I know you were paid for the duration of this trip, so if you leave now, you'd be in breach of contract. It's an agreement you had with my father, not my grandmother.'

She gave him the side-eye. 'Really? You're going to sue me if I leave?'

'Probably not, but I'm under strict instructions from my grandmother to make sure you enjoy your free time on the island until she comes back. I don't know about you, but I don't want to tick her off.' Strictly speaking, that wasn't one hundred percent true, but he was sure that's what she meant when she told him to make sure Jo was all right. And he felt bad for judging her so harshly when she was actually an excellent nurse who had proved her worth today.

It was sufficient for the defiant tilt of Jo's chin to falter a little. 'She's not mad at me?'

'No one is mad at you. So stay, enjoy your vacation.' He moved to help her take her jacket off as proof she wasn't going anywhere.

'I'm not sure I'd feel right lounging around when I'm supposed to be working, with your grandmother in hospital.'

'Well, you can always help me out. I'm running a free clinic on a neighbouring island. An extra pair of hands is always welcome.'

'I suppose…if it means I'm doing something constructive and not self-indulgent…'

'It's a deal then. Get some sleep. We'll be leaving early.' Taylor walked away before she had the chance to change her mind.

It was refreshing to find she had the same work ethic and conscience as he had, even if it didn't fit with the notion he had of a manipulator ingratiating herself with the family. Unless that was what she wanted him to believe… He didn't want to fall for that shtick twice. Spending time running a busy clinic would certainly help him learn more about the sort of person she was, and whether or not he had completely misjudged her after all.

CHAPTER FOUR

ISLAND-HOPPING IN THE sun wasn't something Jo had ever pictured herself being a part of, especially given her financial status, but that's exactly what she was doing. Even though she was going to work, it all seemed very glamorous. However, she'd insisted on wearing her uniform today, so she, and everyone else, would know why she was here. Taylor had chosen a light white cotton shirt teamed with some board shorts for a more casual, and comfortable, look.

'Are you okay?' he asked, helping her out of the boat they'd taken across to Loloma, one of the small neighbouring islands.

'Yes. A bit apprehensive about what lies ahead, I suppose. I've never done anything like this before.'

'You'll be great. Honestly, you'll get as much out of doing this as the community will get from you helping.'

'So you do this a lot?' Jo lifted some of the medical supplies Taylor had unloaded from the boat and followed him across the beach. There was a lot more foliage on this island compared to the one the Stroud family currently resided on, the tree line starting at the far end of the sand and continuing as far as the eye could see. It made her wonder about the people who lived here. How many there were, where they lived, and how they'd feel about her and Taylor landing here.

'When I can. It takes some organising. You know, transport, liaising with the local hospitals, and the community etcetera.'

'At least funding isn't a problem.'

'No. It does have its perks I guess.' He didn't look happy about it and Jo knew he was conflicted over the matter. But she appreciated the effort he went to for the money to make a difference in other people's lives. Not everyone would give their time and energy for something that didn't result in payment or accolades. As he said, the reward for him must've come in helping others. An admirable quality that wasn't in plentiful supply. Certainly not with her ex.

'And the locals don't get upset by outside interference?' She was trying to choose her words carefully, but she wanted to be sure he wasn't seen as some arrogant rich saviour riding in on his horse for the sake of his own ego, even if she knew it wasn't true.

'Trust me, I can be very diplomatic when I

need to be. I only go where I'm sure my services are wanted. So far that hasn't been a problem as people are desperate in some cases for accessible medical care.'

His words satisfied her that she wasn't about to walk into a protest about their arrival on the island and some of the tension left her body.

'And where exactly are we setting up this clinic?' She had yet to see any sign of life, save for the man who'd dropped them off in the boat and was now halfway across the sea in the opposite direction.

Taylor waited until they'd hiked up the trail between the trees to the main 'road', which was essentially a dirt track, to respond. 'At the community centre. Over there.'

A very grand name for the hut that looked as though it had been thrown together using bits of old corrugated iron and planks of wood.

'It looks like it would topple down with one gust of wind.' She doubted the palm leaf roof would keep much rainwater out either.

'We could set up on the beach, but there wouldn't be much protection from the sun, and it could be a long day.'

'It's fine. Just not what I'm used to.' She didn't want to seem churlish, but it was a contrast to the conditions they'd been living in on the neighbouring island. Goodness knew how he got used to this after living his life in privilege, but Jo supposed that was what had pricked his conscience in the first place.

'I don't think someone like you will have a problem fitting in.'

'What's that supposed to mean?' The thought that he saw her as the poor relation immediately put her back up, regardless that it was true.

Taylor's smile neutralised her urge to scowl. 'I mean you're kind and compassionate, and everyone likes you. I don't think it matters where you are, or who you're with, you'll always be welcomed.'

It was a nice thing to say and the compliment put a spring in her step as they made their way over to the hut. 'Well, thank you, kind sir.'

'I mean it. I know we got off to a rocky start but I, er, I've learned not to take people at face value any more. Not everyone is what they seem, but I can see you're genuine, Jo.' It was a heartfelt attempt to build bridges with her, but it also made her wonder about what had happened in the past. Clearly, someone had given him cause to be so defensive, even if she wasn't the one who deserved his wrath.

'It's taken you long enough,' she joked, and managed to make him smile.

'I know. I guess it takes a near death experience with a loved one for me to trust anyone these days.'

'I'm sorry.' She knew exactly how that felt, and despite their differences, she was sorry he'd suffered some sort of betrayal.

'It's not your fault. We, er, just had some trouble a while back with someone getting close to the family and stealing some money. I shouldn't have assumed you were the same.'

'It's okay. When someone lets you down like that, it's difficult to get over, I know.' Although Taylor was referencing the family, his earlier comments, and the fact that he was the only one who'd been suspicious of Jo, led her to believe this was a personal matter for him. Perhaps they had more in common than they'd initially thought, even if he hadn't been left bankrupt by whoever had taken him for a ride.

He gave her a quizzical look, as though wondering what her story was, then appeared to decide to let the matter drop. Likely because he didn't want to go into detail about what had happened to him, and Jo wasn't going to push it, since she wasn't in a hurry to share her experience either.

'Anyway, it's all in the past, and I'm just glad you're here to give a helping hand.' They carried on over to the hut in silence, though it seemed to Jo as though they had made some sort of connection. Even if neither of them were ready to open up just yet.

There was a party of locals inside the community centre waiting to greet them, along with a table full of fresh fruit and snacks.

'Welcome.' A mountain of a man with a beaming smile came and shook their hands enthusiastically.

'You must be Isaac.' Taylor returned the handshake with gusto.

'I'm Jo. I hope you don't mind me tagging along today.'

'Not at all. Are you a doctor too?'

'A nurse. I can give first aid to any minor injuries that might come in.'

'We're very pleased to have you here. Everyone is looking forward to meeting you.' Isaac, whom she assumed was some kind of community leader, appeared to be in charge, or at least had been working with Taylor to make this happen.

He led them over to meet the rest of the group, all dressed in colourful casual wear, which made her feel way overdressed.

'What do you need?' Isaac asked once everyone had been introduced and they'd been furnished with drinks.

'A table and some chairs will do for starters. We might need a private area for examining patients too.' Taylor glanced around the small room, which looked as though it was used for everything from church services to school lessons.

Whilst Isaac and the others rearranged the furniture for their makeshift clinic, Taylor pulled over an old-fashioned free-standing chalkboard. 'We could use this as a screen.'

As he pulled a chair in behind it, Jo began unpacking medical supplies onto one of the empty tables that wasn't currently laden with food.

'Okay, I think we're ready for business.' Taylor took a seat at the table and clapped his hands together.

'Good, because there's a queue forming outside already.' Isaac peered out the door before waving the first patients inside.

Before they knew it the room was crammed with people chatting and helping themselves to refreshments. Jo got the impression this was the way they welcomed everyone to the island and whilst it was a lovely atmosphere, they'd come here to do a job.

Clearly Taylor felt the same way as he got to his feet and banged for attention on the table. 'Hi, everyone. I want to thank you all for coming to our clinic today. Obviously, we want to see as many of you as we can today, so if we could ask you to form some sort of queue it would make this go smoother.'

Everyone stopped and stared, listening to his words, but no one made a move.

Jo sidled up to Taylor. 'Why don't I take names and details and triage here first, then I'll send them back to you.'

'Good idea. Thanks, Jo.' A relieved Taylor touched her lightly on the arm, but it was enough to leave her skin tingling. Reminding her of the moment they'd shared at the waterfall.

She shut down the thoughts capable of making her hot and bothered because she had work to do, and was grateful for it. Otherwise, she would have nothing but Taylor and the memories of him wet and half-naked to occupy her thoughts until Isabelle was back.

'You can button your shirt again, Mary. It's nothing to worry about, but your heart is racing a bit. That's what could be causing the dizzy spells. I'm going to refer you to a specialist on the mainland and they can organise some scans for you.' Taylor couldn't administer any medication here; she would have to have an ECG to see what was going on first, but he could make the referral.

'Thank you, Doctor.' The elderly woman began to rummage in her handbag.

'There's no payment necessary. This is a free clinic.' He'd had to repeat that a lot over the course of the morning. Although they didn't have much, these were proud people who seemed to want to pay for their time today. So far, he'd accumulated quite a collection of food and handmade gifts in kind for treating people today and he didn't want to refuse in case he offended anyone.

'It is just a token of my appreciation,' she said, pulling out a beautiful hand-painted fan.

'Thank you so much.' Taylor accepted it graciously before showing Mary out again. He took a moment to check in with Jo too. She'd done an excellent job of sorting the clinic into something more organised and efficient than he'd ever managed in these sorts of conditions. Since she was able to treat some of the more superficial injuries and ailments, she was sharing the workload too. Though she was beginning to look a little flushed, and no wonder with the lack of air conditioning in the basic facilities they were working in.

'How's it going?' he asked, handing her the fan Mary had just gifted to him.

She took it and immediately began to fan herself. 'Good. A few cuts and sprains to deal with. That's all I can really do with just a first aid kit.'

'I know. It's frustrating, but short of building my own hospital in every one of these areas, that's all we can do in terms of being hands-on. I can diagnose the obvious and make referrals, but in terms of further investigation and ongoing treatment, they have to go to the mainland.' He wished he could do more, but supplies were limited. The most he could do was make donations towards the hospitals themselves, which he did, to pay for more staff and specialised equipment.

'Obviously these people still need your help or else we wouldn't have such a big turnout. I'm sure it's not as easy to go island hopping without your own private helicopter.' She was teasing him, but he appreciated her validation of what he was trying to do in places like this. It gave him the motivation to continue his work, even if it sometimes felt like a drop in the ocean of what was needed.

'I see everyone's been showing their appreciation to you too.' He nodded towards the flower leis and shell necklaces around her neck and decorating the table.

'They're so lovely here. I think we could probably move here permanently and be treated like royalty for the rest of our days.'

'I think I've had my fair share of pampering, but you certainly deserve to be treated like the queen you are.' The idea of just the two of them being out here away from the rest of civilisation was tempting, if not a complete fantasy. At least the simple life wouldn't have him constantly on alert, suspicious that everyone who came into his life was there for nefarious reasons.

Although, it was getting more and more difficult to imagine Jo was anything like his ex. Especially when she looked content with so little. He didn't think all the jewels in the world would put as big a smile on her face as the seashell necklace that she was playing with around her neck.

'Maybe after I've finished here,' she said, getting back to her paperwork.

'So, who have we got next?'

'Michael Reyus, a diabetic. Looks like gout.' She handed him the patient's details with a smile and she looked so at home here, so content, he wished this could have been a permanent arrangement. Sometimes she looked as though she had the weight of the world on her shoulders.

'You need to keep this nice and dry to give it a chance to heal, okay?' Jo finished dressing the nasty cut on her patient's hand.

'Does that mean I can't fish?' The panic in the man's eyes was understandable when it was how he made his living. It was also how he'd injured himself, a slip of the knife when he'd been gutting his catch.

'You could use a plastic bag to keep the water from getting into it. Just be careful you don't get it infected. If there's any sign of swelling, or you have a temperature, make sure to get some medical advice.' She was sorry they wouldn't be here to do a follow-up on the patients they'd met today. In the brief time they'd spent with the locals, she'd got to know and like every one of them. They deserved to have the same medical treatment most people took for granted.

'Thank you.' The relief on his face was surpassed by his gratitude as he shook her hand and left her with a whittled wooden fish. A hobby she hoped he would set aside for a while given his recent history.

'We're going to need a bigger boat to transport all of this back with us. We could open our own souvenir shop,' Taylor commented as he turned the fish over in his hands.

'Well, I'm taking every single gift home. I'll have some lovely memories every time I look at them.'

'I told you it was worth the trip.'

'Indeed, it is, but how do you do it? How do you walk away after? In our line of work, we're used to seeing patients through their treatment. This must feel like setting something in motion and never seeing it through to the conclusion.' Taylor gave her the impression of someone who liked to be in control. She didn't imagine it was easy for him to walk away and absolve himself of any responsibility when he seemed to take on more than any ordinary person could handle on their own.

'It's not ideal, but it's more than these people are currently getting in the way of medical treatment. At least with mobile clinics I can see more patients.' Taylor gathered up more paperwork, obviously trying to help as many people as he could while they were here.

Jo couldn't help but wonder what motivated him, what drove him. Okay, so he wanted the family money to be put to good use, but there was more to it. With no apparent partner of his own, his work seemed to be his life. As though he was running from something else. She should know, when she'd been doing the same for the past two years.

'I'm sure they're all very grateful. I know I am for you letting me take part.' It showed a lot of trust on his part. Especially after their initial meet. For someone who liked to keep a tight rein, he was opening up his world and putting his faith in her medical abilities along with his own.

'Help! I need some help!' A man burst in through the door, rushing towards them carrying a screaming child in his arms, blood everywhere.

'Get him over here.' Taylor cleared one of the tables so they could lay the young boy down, whilst Jo rushed to chivvy everyone else out of the hall.

'This is an emergency. If you could all just give the boy some privacy and wait outside until we treat him, it would be greatly appreciated.' Although the waiting patients were all peering over her shoulder, trying to get a better view of what was happening, Jo managed to herd them all outside.

She closed the door and rushed back to see what she could do to help.

'What happened?' Taylor asked the father as he stripped off the child's bloodied shirt.

Jo grabbed Taylor's medical bag along with a first aid kit and carried the supplies over.

'He was wrestling with his brother. We've told them time and time again that someone's going to get hurt, but they don't listen...'

'There are lacerations all over his face and body.' Taylor peered closer. 'I think there's glass in some of the wounds.'

'He fell through the glass table. It shattered. I didn't know whether to pull the glass shards out or leave them where they are.' The father was understandably distraught over his son's injuries. Although the cuts could be superficial, there was always that chance that a shard could penetrate vital organs or arteries, causing the patient to bleed out. They would have to do a careful examination of every wound.

'Did he lose consciousness at any time? Any vomiting?'

'No.'

Hopefully that meant he hadn't suffered a concussion during the fall.

'What's his name?' Jo asked, setting out antiseptic and gauze to dress the cuts.

'Jack. I'm his father, Dessie.'

'Okay, Dessie. We're going to have to clean and dress his injuries. You can take a seat or wait outside.' She knew they would work better if he wasn't standing over their shoulder.

'I—I think I'll wait outside. Get some fresh air.'

'We'll give him some pain relief to help him. Does he have any allergies we should be aware of?'

'No.'

'Don't go, Dad.' Jack reached for his father, but Jo stood between them.

'We're going to take good care of you, Jack.' Then, turning to Dessie, she added, 'We'll come and get you if we need you.'

'I'll be right outside, son. The doctor's going to make sure you're all right.' Dessie dropped a quick kiss on his son's head and left one last lingering look before he walked out, hands on his head, torn about whether or not he was doing the right thing.

'Jack, we're going to have to clean all your cuts and make sure we get any glass out. It's going to sting a bit. We'll give you something to help with the pain, but I need you to be brave, okay?' Taylor spoke softly to the terrified child before he did anything. It was always a sign of a good doctor when they took time to explain to the patient what they were doing, no matter what age they were dealing with.

He gave the boy some pain relief, asked him about his favourite wrestlers, and generally won over his trust before attempting to treat him. Jo admired his compassion, and the understanding of how terrified the child was in the circumstances. Honesty and kindness were always the best policy with children. Trauma wasn't easily forgotten, as she could testify all these years later.

If her parents had only explained to her at an early age, believed in her that she could process and deal with it, then news of her adoption wouldn't have felt like such a betrayal. Finding out for herself when she was practically an adult had made her question not only who she was, but who she'd been living with for her entire life. Trust, once lost, wasn't easily given again.

Taylor handed her a pair of tweezers, showing he had faith enough in her to let her do the important work with him. Carefully, and methodically, they set to work cleaning the numerous cuts, and extracting the bits of glass embedded within.

'There are a few here that are going to need stitches.' Taylor rummaged in his medical bag to find the necessary supplies and set to work closing the larger wound sites.

Jack winced.

'You're being so brave,' she assured him, brushing his dark hair from his forehead. It made her think of all the times she'd fallen and been patched up by her mother. Her soothing words a comfort. Their bond so strong, once upon a time. Now, even though they were living in the same house, they felt like strangers forced together.

'We need to turn you over, Jack. We'll be as gentle as we can.' Taylor's instructions brought her back into the room, and the needs of their patient.

He'd suffered the most injuries to his arms and face, but there was always the chance he could have landed on some glass during the fall. They gently rolled him onto his side at first and Jo slid a towel onto the table to try and cushion him a little bit as they moved him onto his front. Jack's little cry of discomfort struck deep at her heart, wishing she could make everything better for him.

She wasn't a parent, but that natural instinct to protect a vulnerable child came to the fore. Not for the first time she thought about the parents who'd given her away. Had they done so for her own benefit, or had it been a selfish act? She'd never know because she'd since learned of their passing. The denial of her true identity for so long preventing her from ever finding out or getting to know her birth family. More reasons she didn't think she could ever forgive those who'd lied to her throughout her childhood.

'I think there's a big piece of glass stuck in here. I could do with some better light to see what I'm doing…' Taylor was crouched down, studying a deep gash near Jack's spine.

Jo knew if there was something left in there it could cause severe damage to nerves, or organs, and being so close to the spine could even result in paralysis.

She rushed around the room making sure all the curtains were wide open, then grabbed a small table lamp from the back of the room. Plugging it in to an extension cord, she carried it over and held it close to the wound so Taylor could see better.

'Thanks.' He took a moment to flash her a grateful smile and in that moment she felt a bond between them. They were working as a team. Something they fell into as easily as they had when Isabelle had been injured. She wasn't used to that, having been on her own for so long, concentrating on her own survival. It was nice to have company again, someone working towards the same goals. She could easily get used to it. Though that was where the danger lay. Any time she relied on anyone, they let her down, betrayed her trust and left her broken.

'It's deep in there. Ideally we'd get him to hospital…' Taylor didn't finish his sentence, but she understood what he meant.

In a hospital environment they'd be able to numb the area before attempting to extract the glass, but they didn't have that luxury here. Even if they had the means to transfer him immediately, one wrong move, a bump in the road, and there was a chance of doing further serious injury. Perhaps paralysis, or even death, depending on how deep the glass was, and how close it was to vital body parts. This one in particular was too close to the spine to take a chance. Even removing it ran the risk of doing more damage, though she was sure Taylor would do his utmost to avoid that.

'I'll open the wound a little more so you can get inside there.' She set the lamp down on the table so it was still lighting up the important area for them to see where they were working.

'Jack, this is going to hurt a little, but there's some glass in there that we need to get out quickly. I need you to be a big boy and be as still as you can. It'll all be over soon, then we can bring your dad back in.' Jo gave him some warning before they began the procedure, knowing it wasn't going to be pleasant.

She pulled the skin slightly apart so Taylor could get inside the wound with the tweezers, earning a cry from Jack.

'I'm so sorry. We'll be as quick as we can.' She

watched Taylor dig in with a grimace, but when he got hold of the shard and gently eased it out, she was able to breathe again.

'All done,' Taylor announced, the relief evident in his voice as the tension seemed to leave his shoulders.

'You're so brave.' Jo leaned in and whispered in Jack's ear, suddenly tearful for everything he'd endured.

Taylor moved quickly then to close the site and dress it to prevent any infection and Jo was able to go and get Dessie to reunite him with his son. 'You can come in and see him now. Just be very careful, he's going to be tender.'

Jack sobbed as his dad came in.

'Is he going to be okay?' he asked Taylor, who was cleaning the boy up and wiping away as much blood as he could.

'I'll send some painkillers home with him but he's going to have to rest up and give those cuts a chance to heal over. I'll see if Isaac can arrange transport home for you both. We don't want to move him any more than is necessary.'

'I can go home?'

'Yes, Jack, but no more wrestling for a while. Okay?' Jo was sure she wasn't the only one in the room who would've given him a great big hug if he wasn't so delicate right now.

'You're going to have to keep an eye on him tonight, Dessie. The first sign of a temperature, or any nausea, get him to the hospital. Actually...' Taylor pulled out his phone. 'Call me. I can come here, or get you to the hospital myself. I'm only a phone call away.'

'Thank you.' Dessie looked relieved and thankful as he took down Taylor's contact information.

Jo knew Taylor would keep his word and get help here the second it was needed, even if it meant calling in a few favours from his father. At least he wasn't someone who would prioritise his principles over someone's health. It was good to see he was a man of action, as well as words. The more time she spent with him, the less he seemed like the rest of his family, and the more there was to appreciate about him. He wasn't just a philanthropic rich kid who looked good in a pair of wet shorts. Taylor Stroud was a true humanitarian, a man she was glad she'd got to know, and someone she was going to miss when she went home.

Uh-oh!

Between them all, they managed to lift Jack into the back of Isaac's truck, with strict instructions from Taylor to go slowly. It wasn't the first emergency he'd had to deal with in such a remote area, or even the first time he'd run a clinic jointly with anyone. However, it was the first time he'd done it all with Jo, and he had to say, he kind of liked it.

Of course, he wished young Jack hadn't gone through such a harrowing time, but Jo had been good at keeping him calm. They'd also got through more patients than he'd expected because they'd been able to share the work. She might be used to working one-on-one these days, but she'd been more than capable of organising and triaging the patients to make his working day go as smooth as possible in the circumstances. Although he ultimately preferred to be the one in control whenever he did one of these trips, he could see the benefits of having a partner. At work at least. In terms of his personal life, it would be a long time before he'd trust anyone enough to let them into his private world and run the risk of being hurt again.

Taylor didn't think he'd ever be able to have a proper relationship again even if he met someone he wanted to have in his life. He'd be waiting, looking for signs that something wasn't quite right, expecting that final devastating blow to his heart. His ex had made him that way—distrusting, wary and unable to completely give himself to another person.

He'd believed he'd found someone with common interests and passions, a woman he would possibly spend the rest of his life with, and she'd been lying and scheming the whole time. The happiness he'd felt had been fake. It gave him some insight into the way his mother had felt when her marriage to his father had ended so cruelly and abruptly.

Perhaps he'd ignored any signs that something was wrong in his own relationship because he'd been so desperate to find the security and stability he hadn't had from his family. To be with someone who accepted him for who he was. Imogen had pretended to understand him, to share common passions and interests, and he'd foolishly accepted it as fact when all along it had been a lie. All so she could get her hands on his money. It was so cliché, and he should have seen it a mile away, but he'd been so blinded by love. Now it would take a miracle for him to ever feel that way about someone again.

Taylor wondered if that was the family curse. That because of their wealth, it wouldn't be possible to ever find someone who could see past it. The only thing he could rely on, the only good thing in his life now, was his work. It was a pleasant change to have Jo here helping him with it when it was usually something of a lone experience.

They managed to see a couple of the more urgent patients before they started to lose the light and began to wrap things up. By the time Isaac came back, they were ready to leave.

'Did Jack and Dessie get home safely?' he

asked, before Isaac even had time to shut off the engine.

'Yes. They're fine, and very grateful that you were here today to help. I wish we had you permanently.' Isaac clapped him on the back. A hearty thump given with genuine affection and appreciation.

'And I wish we could do more, I really do, but we have to get back to Bensak.'

Jo nodded as she joined them outside the hall carrying some of their medical supplies. 'Do we just meet the boat back on the shore?'

'Oh, the boat won't be coming back tonight,' Isaac informed them with a grin.

'Pardon?'

'Why not?' Jo sounded as anxious as he was suddenly feeling at the news.

He was exhausted, hungry and had been looking forward to heading back to unwind. Now he was as tense as the first night he'd arrived on the family retreat.

'It's too dark now, and the wind is getting up. The weather changes quickly here. There will be no boat until the morning.'

Taylor's mouth dropped open, no words seeming to come, whilst Jo looked visibly pained at the thought of remaining here with him for the night. 'But where are we going to stay?'

'I have a bed in my house you are welcome to

use.' Isaac's offer did little to lessen the abject horror on Jo's face.

'We can't share a bed. Taylor, can't you do something? You could get us a helicopter out of here.' There was a rising sense of panic in Jo's voice, and though he could understand her anxiety about being stuck here with him for the night, he couldn't justify making an SOS call like that.

'If it's going to be dark and stormy, I don't really want to put someone's life in jeopardy simply because we might be a bit uncomfortable for one night. I'm sure we can manage.'

He could see Jo churning everything over in her mind and gradually coming to accept this was happening. 'Where are we going to sleep?'

'If you don't want to camp out on the beach, we could just pull up a few chairs here. Would that be okay, Isaac?'

'Of course. I can bring you some blankets, if you're happy to stay here.' Isaac look relieved they'd no longer be his responsibility, and they weren't going to insist on trying to get off the island.

'I wouldn't say happy...' Jo mumbled and dropped the bags she was carrying, making it clear she was reluctant, if resigned, to the change of plans.

'We'll have shelter, there's plenty of food and drink left, and on the plus side, we'll be able to check Jack over in the morning again.' He was trying to look at the positives. It was more than a lot of people had, and it wouldn't be the first time he'd had to rough it. It was ironic that it wasn't him that was struggling with the idea of leaving luxury behind for one night. Unless it was more about who she was stranded here with.

They'd clashed at first, but they'd also had some bonding moments over his grandmother, and the patients they'd treated. He didn't think she was still holding a grudge over his rude attitude that first night, but there was obviously something more than the lack of Egyptian cotton sheets concerning her. For him, the increasing concern was the amount of time they were spending together. He was becoming increasingly close to Jo, and if he was honest, spending the night here with her didn't seem as much of a disaster to him as it clearly did to her. Which was a red flag in itself…

They had a lot in common, including their medical backgrounds, and, he suspected, their need to keep their personal lives private. He knew nothing of her, or her life, beyond caring for his grandmother, but he found himself wanting to find out more. All signs that he needed to be careful. He'd been there before, and the last time a woman had piqued his interest, he'd been left devastated by betrayal. Taylor had to make sure his professional admiration for Jo didn't stray into something more dangerous.

CHAPTER FIVE

Jo WASN'T USUALLY one to panic. She was used to being calm in a crisis, a prerequisite in her line of work. This felt different. Out of her comfort zone.

It wasn't a life-threatening situation, and perhaps she was overreacting, but the thought of being alone with Taylor all night was giving her heart palpitations. After spending all day in his company she needed to retreat back into her own space and put some distance between them so she could gather her thoughts, remember all the reasons she was here and why liking him was a bad idea.

She couldn't trust her judgement any more. Certainly not when it came to men. Steve had destroyed everything. Not just her business, and her sense of security, but he'd taken away the very essence of who she was. Jo Kirkham was no longer a successful businesswoman content in both her professional and home life. Now she was an employee, a lodger and completely at the mercy of others. It wasn't an ideal situation for someone who thought they could no longer trust another soul.

Besides, if she'd been duped by people she thought were her parents her whole life, as well as a man she'd given herself completely to, she had to be careful about getting close to new people. Her heart was a liar and not to be trusted. She was managing to survive now, but she didn't think she could withstand another betrayal. There was too much risk involved in letting a stranger further into her life.

Without other people or distractions, being stuck here together in this small hall was only going to force them to get to know each other better. Since the more he revealed about himself, the more reasons there were to like him, she was worried to say the least.

'Thank you.' Jo took the bundle of blankets Isaac's wife, Elizabeth, had very kindly brought them. He and his children followed behind bringing cushions and trailing a mattress with them.

'It might be more comfortable than those hard chairs, for one of you at least. It can get cold at night. We've brought you some water and food too. There should be enough to see you through the night at least.' Isaac threw the mattress down in the middle of the floor and once the children had finished hitting each other with the cushions, they arranged them on the mattress.

Jo felt ashamed about her reaction to having to stay the night when they were all being so hospitable.

'You really shouldn't have gone to all this trouble, but thank you.' Taylor shook Isaac's hand, showing their appreciation. They could easily have been left to fend for themselves, but as Taylor had reminded her, they had food and shelter and should be grateful.

'It's the least we can do for you after you looked after our little community so well today. I'll let you know the minute we can get someone to take you back home in the morning. We'll let you get settled for the night.' Isaac rounded up his children and ushered them back out as noisily as they'd entered the hall.

'Thanks again.' Jo gave Elizabeth an awkward hug, squashing the bale of bedding between their bodies as she did so, but she was reluctant to let them all go. As soon as they walked out it was just her and Taylor left here alone until morning.

'They're lovely people, aren't they?' Taylor was smiling to himself as he closed the door and sealed them in the hall for the night.

'Yes. I hope I didn't come across as a petulant, spoiled tourist. It was just a shock to find we weren't going to be able to leave the island.'

'I'm sure they understand. Although I get the impression they'd be more than happy for us both to stay here and become part of the community permanently.' Taylor's words, though in jest, made her shiver.

There was something about the thought of them living and working together here for ever that was more than tempting. She had to cling to the recent traumatic memories of doing just that with Steve to prevent her from getting carried away with the fairy tale again.

'I think one night will be more than enough.' Jo set about making the bed up with the blankets Isaac and his family had provided, whilst Taylor concerned himself with the contents of the foil-covered dishes they'd brought.

'Mmm, chicken,' he said, munching down on a drumstick. The barbecue aroma began to waft across the room, making Jo's stomach rumble and reminding her she hadn't eaten for a while.

Jo opened another of the food containers to reveal a vegetable rice dish. She grabbed a fork and dug in.

'You want some?' She offered the spicy accompaniment to her dining companion and they did a swap so she could help herself to some of the delicious-smelling chicken.

They stood, eating directly out of the dishes, grinning at each other, until they'd had their fill.

'You'd think we'd never seen food,' Taylor remarked as they stacked the empty dishes on the table.

'We must've been hungry.'

'It's all the excitement that does it. That adrenaline rush when an emergency comes in always makes me hungry afterwards.'

'Does it happen often? I'm not sure I'd like to be stuck in the middle of nowhere with a life-or-death emergency with everyone relying on me.' Today had been different. Although Jack had suffered a serious injury, the pressure hadn't been solely on her to save his life. With her usual clientele, as soon as they developed any health complications the hospital was the first point of contact. In places like this that luxury wasn't available.

'Now and then. It's part of the job, isn't it?'

'I guess so. Don't you ever just want something more secure? To settle down?' Despite everything she'd gone through, Jo mourned that version of her, so full of optimism and certainty that she'd found happiness with Steve. Like most people, she'd thought that her future was all set because she had a partner to share her life with. Now all she wanted was a permanent position and a house to call her own again. Peace.

'I could have that if I wanted. I did, once upon a time. It's not all it's cracked up to be.'

'Oh?'

Taylor hesitated before he continued, as though

pondering whether or not to share any more with her. He pulled up one of the plastic chairs and sat down.

'I, er, did the whole eight to five in a GP practice, had my own place, and a steady relationship. Imogen was a director of a local charity, and I thought we had the same world view. We talked about setting up our own charity project providing medical services to disadvantaged people abroad. She even left her job to help set it up. We'd agreed I'd keep working in the meantime, and I was funding all of it.'

Jo didn't like the sound of where this was heading, or the dark shadow that was beginning to creep over Taylor's handsome features as he spoke about it.

'I'm guessing it didn't work out the way you expected it to?'

'That's an understatement. The whole thing was fake. There was no charity. Unless you count the Imogen Potter designer handbag fund. She'd been pocketing all the money, and when I found out she just laughed, said I could afford it.'

'That's terrible. Did you report her?'

'What was the point? She was right—I could afford it, and dragging her through the courts wasn't going to change anything. It was my heart, my trust, that had taken a bigger hammering than my wallet.' He gave Jo a half-hearted smile that did nothing to hide the hurt he was clearly still feeling over the incident. It was understandable when she was struggling two years on to forgive her ex for everything he'd done, and she wasn't sure she ever would. Even when she had paid off her debt and moved on, she knew that betrayal would live on inside her. That broken trust left an indelible mark and changed a person.

'I know how that feels…'

'Oh? Do tell. I don't want to be the only sad sack running away from my problems out here.' Taylor leaned forward, resting his head on his hand, batting his eyelashes at her.

He did make her laugh.

Jo took a deep breath. It wasn't something she'd shared with anyone unless they'd needed to know. Like bank officials and employees, and all the other people she'd had to face when her ex skipped out of town.

She pulled up a chair and sat down too. 'I used to have my own business, with my partner, Steve. We had a lovely house, and I pictured us raising a family together.'

'And he didn't?'

'Obviously not. He did a runner, and hasn't been seen since.'

'And the business?'

'It's gone. That's why I'm back working as a private nurse. So I think I win the sob story contest.' She tried to make light of it because she didn't want him to see how much she was still hurting over the whole ordeal. It wasn't going to define who she was, but it was still impacting on her, and would until she was able to get back her independence.

'I'm sorry,' he said eventually.

'It hasn't been easy for either of us, but hey, we're not the bad people in either scenario. We're the good guys.' Something she had realised over the course of these past two days was that Taylor most definitely was one of the good guys. Even if he didn't always let people see it at first.

She could have sworn he muttered something like, "I hope so."

Taylor watched as Jo settled into the hard plastic chairs, rearranging the cushions below her head into a makeshift pillow.

'What are you doing?'

'I'm going to sleep. It's been a long day. You can take the mattress.'

'Absolutely not. You can't think much of me if you think I'm the sort of man who'd expect you to sleep in a chair while I'm lounging in a bed.'

'I think a lot of you. That's why you're having the bed. You organised this clinic. I'm here on your dime. You're about a foot taller than I am, and I can sleep anywhere. Just get into bed, Taylor.' With that, she rolled onto her side, her back to him. Preventing him from extending the argument.

Since it didn't make any sense for both of them to spend an uncomfortable night trying to sleep on two chairs pulled together, he resigned himself to taking the comfier option. Even though he was embarrassed about doing so.

He pulled off his shirt with a sigh, kicked off his shoes and climbed under the covers. Dealing with small, remote communities, working in difficult conditions, was easier for him than managing personal relationships. Regardless that Jo wasn't a girlfriend, he'd involved himself in her relationship with his grandmother. That meant she was part of his life now too. At least for the duration of this New Year's trip.

He lay staring into darkness, his mind working overtime thinking about everything that had happened since he arrived on the island. Sometimes his thoughts drifting back to Imogen and how foolish he'd been in trusting her so completely. Then he wondered about Jo and what she'd told him about her relationship. If she had suffered the way he had.

He drifted in and out of consciousness, the wind howling outside keeping him from falling into a deep sleep. The rattle of the loose windows became louder and louder until he was fully awake. He sat up and pummelled his pillow into submission in the hope of getting a more comfortable sleep, only to catch sight of Jo curled up in the corner. She had the blanket pulled up to her chin but her teeth were chattering from the cold.

'Jo? Are you all right?'

'I'm fine,' she said, shivering.

'Get into this bed before you end up with hypothermia,' he insisted, glad when she rushed over and climbed in beside him.

Her whole body was shaking as she curled up into a foetal position next to him.

'You're freezing. Why didn't you tell me?'

'And admit I needed your help?' she chattered through her grin.

'Come here, you silly sod.' Taylor forgot all of his concerns in light of her plight. He put an arm around her and pulled her close into him.

'Next you'll be telling me to strip off to generate more body heat.'

Her jest in the midst of her obvious discomfort made him chuckle. 'Feel free. Or we could just pull the covers up around us.'

Despite the joking around, her comment had sparked images and feelings that were definitely not appropriate for someone trying to rescue a damsel in distress. Then she mischievously pressed her cold nose and frozen feet against his body to jolt him back into the moment.

'I think I can feel my toes again,' she said once she stopped shaking.

'Good.'

She was curled around his body now, her head in the crook of his shoulder, and her arm splayed across his chest. It should've felt uncomfortable both physically, and emotionally, but it wasn't. When Jo's breathing became steady, her chest rising and falling against him, for some reason, Taylor felt at peace. As though he'd found a missing piece of himself.

Instead of freaking out about the implications of that, or concerns about how vulnerable he was making himself, he began to drift into a peaceful slumber.

Jo became increasingly aware of the hard body she was pressed against as she came to. She should've scrambled out of bed to safety, away from Taylor and the threat he posed to her equilibrium. But she didn't.

It was such a pleasant sensation waking up next to him, feeling safe and secure in his arms, that she was reluctant to leave his embrace. He'd been her source of warmth and comfort in the night, and now he was the romantic fantasy she'd been missing in her life. She'd rebelled against the idea of getting involved with anyone else since her ex had done the dirty on her, but Taylor was reminding her of the good things to be found in a relationship. Even if he wasn't aware of it.

Even if he could never be the one for her.

There were so many things Jo didn't know about him, and she could never dare risk her fragile heart on someone so emotionally closed off. She should remember the first night they'd met, when he'd been so cold, instead of thinking about how she'd shared his warmth last night. He wasn't any more settled in life than she was, and could never bring her the peace of mind she longed for.

Maybe someday she might learn to trust again, and let someone into her life. For now she simply wanted to enjoy the feel of Taylor beneath her, and pretend that this was real.

Perhaps sensing her awake, he began to stir, but Jo continued to feign sleep for as long as she could.

He stretched and yawned, finally forcing her to relinquish her hold on him.

'Morning,' he said sleepily, his eyes still dazed with sleep.

She turned her face up to greet him and before she knew what was happening, he had bent to give her a brief kiss on the mouth. They both froze, staring at each other now wide-eyed at the realisation of what had just happened. However, rather than freaking out and reclaiming her personal space, Jo found herself leaning in for more.

Taylor accepted the invitation and before they knew it, they were in a passionate embrace.

So much for not getting too close...

Lips crushed against lips, arms wrapped around one another, they lost themselves in the passion that had suddenly awakened between them. As though it had been there all this time bubbling beneath the surface and the intimacy of sharing a bed together had given them permission to release it. To embrace this desire neither knew the other had been harbouring.

Jo groaned against him, her brain too befuddled by the taste of him, the feel of him against her, to think clearly. Taylor merely responded by grabbing her backside and pulling her into his ever-hardening body. It was gratifying to feel his arousal pressed against her, confirming this wasn't just a case of mistaken identity. That he hadn't simply woken up in a daze and kissed her believing her to be someone else. Taylor wanted her, and heaven help her, she wanted him too.

All of those issues that had been holding her back from getting involved with another man seemed to evaporate in the face of her need for him. The only thing that mattered right now was how he was making her feel. Wanted. Wanting.

The practicalities of giving into temptation, or how it would affect the rest of their time on the island didn't enter her head. As though she was purposely blocking them out to indulge this erotic fantasy. Until there was a knock on the door and Isaac called in from outside.

'Are you awake in there?'

The second the real world broke through the erotic haze, Jo practically bounced out of bed. Putting some much-needed distance between her and Taylor, though wrenching herself away hadn't erased the memory of him. He was still imprinted on her lips.

'Yes,' Taylor shouted back, his voice gruff.

Jo couldn't even bear to look at him, her skin flushed with embarrassment as well as arousal. She hadn't just lowered her defences, she'd blasted right through them in her desperation to have him. Clearly her body was still craving that intimacy with a partner, even if her head was telling her it was a bad idea. Next time that voice needed to shout a little louder to make sure it was heard. Goodness knew what Taylor would think of her when she'd been about to give herself so willingly to him. He didn't know her well enough to understand this type of behaviour wasn't the norm for her. Which also made it so unnerving. What was it about him that had made her act so out of character? Her head wasn't usually so easily turned by a handsome face. Perhaps it was the knowledge that he had a good heart, making him as attractive on the inside as he was on the outside, that had captured her attention. Whatever it was, she couldn't let it happen again. There was no happy ending to be had here, and if she did ever dare to venture into a relationship, it was going to be with someone she could trust to deliver that.

Not only was Taylor part of the family that employed her, but by his own admission, he didn't want to settle down. He was scarred by his own past relationships, always on the move. Those were not the qualities needed in her ideal man.

'Good morning. I hope you slept okay?' Isaac peered in around the door, checking the coast was clear for him to come in.

Thankfully his good manners had prevented him from walking in on something that would have mortified all of them. As it was, Jo felt the need to keep herself busy folding up the blanket she'd been using last night so she didn't have to face him.

'Like babies,' Taylor lied on her behalf.

She was glad of it. A man like Isaac would have blamed himself if they'd said they'd been cold and uncomfortable, regardless that he'd offered hospitality at his own home. Now Jo realised why she'd been so afraid of sharing a bed with Taylor in the first place. Deep down that attraction towards him had obviously been building and she must've known it subconsciously. Although the discovery that she had feelings for Taylor was unexpected, she could take steps now to avoid being alone with him. The other problem was that he was aware of it now too.

'If you're ready to leave, the boat is here. Of course, you're welcome to stay and have breakfast first—'

'No. We can leave now.' Taylor cut off Isaac's invitation, and though Jo would be glad to escape their almost indiscretion, his eagerness to go was a tad jarring.

She might regret acting on her impulses, but it didn't do her self-esteem much good to find out the feeling was reciprocated. It was possible he'd simply reacted like any other hot-blooded man waking up to a woman in his bed. Any woman. It didn't mean he was attracted to her the same way she was to him. Despite her decision to pretend nothing had happened, the thought that their early morning smooch hadn't been as special as she imagined was a bitter pill to swallow.

Taylor was grateful for the noisy boat engine making conversation impossible. Even if he and Jo were sitting as far apart as could be in the tiny space available.

He'd messed up.

Disoriented, disarmed and half asleep, he'd reacted to the sight of Jo next to him in bed before he'd engaged his brain. If he'd taken time to think about what he was doing he'd have remembered he was supposed to be objective about her presence. Not an active participant.

It hadn't helped that she'd kissed him back with abandon, lighting a fire inside him that had taken some time to extinguish. Even now he was worried that if she as much as smiled at him it would spark straight back to life. Not that she'd glanced in his direction since Isaac had walked in. No doubt regretting the incident as much as he had. He'd ducked out to check in with Jack before they headed for the boat, giving them both some time out from the pressure cooker they'd found themselves in.

The problem was he regretted complicating things between them, but not the kiss itself. It was good to know there was still a passion inside him for more than his work. After Imogen, he'd thought that part of him had died, with no interest in the opposite sex. Yet that had been disproved by how close he'd come to Jo in just a matter of days, despite all of his reservations. Although now he knew how she felt in his arms, how responsive she was to his touch, it was going to be difficult to forget.

'Thank you.' He handed the skipper a handsome tip for his trouble as the boat came to rest in the shallows, then helped Jo out.

Even that simple contact now had the ability to

spark his body to life and he wondered if it was going to be like that every time, and how he was going to stand it. They still had days left on the island. Time to fill, and no place to hide. A ticking time bomb he was afraid would explode with devastating consequences, leaving multiple casualties, and no way back.

He wasn't used to feeling this helpless to his desires. Since the split with Imogen, the opposite sex hadn't held much fascination for him. Betrayal by one woman had erected barriers around his heart to repel everyone else who might be capable of causing him the same pain. He'd channelled all of his energy and passion into his work, with no interest beyond a passing glance at the opposite sex. Until now.

This chemistry he had with Jo had managed to break through those defences. It seemed all-consuming, penetrating his thoughts at inconvenient times, and distracting him from his usual focus. All for what? It couldn't go anywhere. She was his grandmother's nurse, recovering from her own emotional wounds, and only in his life through circumstance. They were such different people, from contrasting backgrounds, and they could never work as a couple. That's why it was such a bad idea to even think about getting involved. It could only end badly, and they'd both had enough painful endings for one lifetime.

He hoped now they were back on the island they would both remember that.

With their equipment on their backs, they schlepped through the water, and made their way back up the sand bank towards the villa. Jo suddenly stopped and turned to face him, her lips pursed into a straight line.

'Look, before we get to the house, I think we should talk about this morning.' It was clear by the look on her face it wasn't a subject she was comfortable discussing, though they both knew it was necessary if they were going to move past it.

'I'm sorry. I shouldn't have kissed you like that.'

'I think we're both to blame, but that's not the point.' He swore her cheeks went pink at the mere mention of it and he wondered briefly if she had been as unaffected as she was trying to project. 'I want to make it clear I'm not looking for anything...romantic.'

'Nor am I.'

'Good. The last thing I want is to jump into a relationship with another man I know nothing about. Or with anyone, actually. Maybe I'll become a nun...'

'Now, that would be a shame. You definitely don't kiss like a nun.'

She was blushing now, and regardless of his intention to try and put the moment of madness behind them, Taylor couldn't help but push her buttons some more. Perhaps because he was sure the immediate danger was over. Jo was no more interested in a relationship than he was. And there was just a satisfaction to be had in knowing that perhaps she'd enjoyed the kissing as much as he had. No matter how unexpected, or inconvenient it was to both of them. And he wanted to test his theory.

'We both got a little carried away,' Jo admitted.

'Oh? So you were into it? That puts things in a very different light.'

'I don't see how. We kissed. We shouldn't have. End of story.'

He took a step closer, saw her nostrils flare and her jaw clench. 'Why not? We're both adults, single and clearly have chemistry. What harm is there in a little kiss?'

Taylor was treading on dangerous ground. One wrong step and he knew he'd be in trouble too, but he couldn't seem to help himself. Some invisible force was driving him on, desperate to touch her again, to feel that same sense of abandon he'd experienced upon waking. They were attracted to one another and if neither of them was interested in anything beyond the physical, maybe it was worth exploring. Just because they weren't going to live happily ever after together, it didn't mean they had to ignore this new feeling of desire creeping in on them.

He reached out and caught a strand of her hair dancing in the wind. Her eyes fluttered shut as though she was anticipating the kiss, and called his bluff. Now it was he who was on the back foot, his teasing having backfired, because he was becoming flushed and bothered.

'There you are!'

They'd been so caught up in each other they'd been unaware of his father approaching. Taylor dropped his hand and stepped away from Jo.

'Yes, we're just heading back to the house to get washed and changed, Dad.' At least then they could retreat to opposite ends of the villa and he could get a cold shower. Something that would hopefully wash away this desperation he'd suddenly developed to keep touching and kissing Jo.

'I'm sure you've both had a tough night. We're just glad you're back in one piece. That's why we've organised lunch later this afternoon for you down at the beach.'

'That's really not necessary, Mr Stroud.' Jo had already started walking again, understandably keen to get away from him.

He felt ashamed for the teasing, for making her uncomfortable and for causing even more trouble.

'It's all sorted. Everyone wants to hear what you've been up to.'

Taylor exchanged a loaded look with Jo. A silent agreement that *no one* would hear exactly what that entailed.

'Dad, it's been a long couple of days. We're exhausted.'

'Oh, don't be a spoil-sport, Taylor. We need some excitement, something to talk about other than your grandmother's health to lighten the mood. I want to hear all about your adventures. So we'll see you both down at the beach bar in an hour.' Clearly, his father wasn't going to take no for an answer. He jogged away without even offering to carry any of their bags.

'Sorry.' He apologised to Jo again, although this one wasn't his fault. 'It looks as though we're both required to attend. He's very persuasive.'

'It must run in the family.' Jo walked away before he could figure out if she meant that as a good thing or a bad thing.

CHAPTER SIX

JO LET THE multiple shower heads in the luxury shower blast her in the vain hope they would wash away those inappropriate feelings she was beginning to have towards Taylor. A few words, the slightest touch, and her body was begging for more from him. She'd sworn off men after Steve, a relationship the last thing on her mind when she'd been fighting just to stay afloat. Now her libido was reminding her that she had other needs.

'Get yourself together, Jo.'

So far the self-motivation talks hadn't been doing much good, when all the reasons she shouldn't want him went out the window the second she looked into those gorgeous brown eyes. But there was no future for them as a couple. Come the New Year they'd be going their own ways, probably in completely different directions.

But he's so hot...

That coquettish little voice in her head swooned, making a mockery of the strong, independent woman she'd been up until recently. Now she was expected to spend the rest of the day with Taylor and his family, instead of being allowed to avoid him so she could make an attempt to get those defences back in place.

When her skin was in danger of either turning wrinkly, or being flayed from her body, she shut off the shower and grabbed a towel. A perusal of her meagre wardrobe left her a little deflated. She hadn't packed to impress, never expecting to be socialising with the family outside of her duties to Isabelle. These were people to whom money was no object. The idea of getting their clothes second hand unthinkable, but she'd had to be frugal these last couple of years. Charity shops and preloved sites online had become her lifeline. Hopefully her dress code wouldn't draw any negative attention, or *any* attention in fact. She'd be content to simply blend into the background. That's why her uniform was more of a security blanket. It rendered her invisible a lot of the time, but today that wasn't going to be an option.

She supposed it hadn't proved to be the barrier she'd hoped for yesterday anyway.

In the end she decided she wanted to be comfortable in the sun rather than attempting any sort of formality. She chose a light cotton sundress with tie strings at the shoulders. It was a cheery lemon colour with little sprigs of lavender embroidered all over. A bargain find in one of her local charity shop haunts, which looked as though it had never been worn. It mightn't be high fashion, or cost the price of a month's wages, but it should keep her cool. Ironic when she'd been shivering only hours ago. That's what had caused all the trouble. If she hadn't climbed in beside Taylor, they might not have succumbed to temptation in the first place.

She slipped on a pair of strappy white sandals and brushed out her hair. It would dry in the sun. There was no need to spend hours styling it because this wasn't a date. This was lunch with her employer and his family. She didn't have to impress anyone, merely get through it.

That's what she told herself as she made her way down to the beach, not daring to wait around for company. With any luck she could plonk herself in a corner somewhere, well away from temptation.

A hope that was quickly extinguished when she heard footsteps running up behind her and turned around to find Taylor beaming at her. 'Are you ready for this?'

'No.'

'Don't worry. We're just there to provide some entertainment.'

'That's really not helping, Taylor.' She rolled her eyes at him, trying not to be swayed by the sight of him in his leaf print, short-sleeved shirt and linen trousers. He looked so relaxed and smelled fresh and clean. Jo was doing her best not to imagine him in the shower, even though his hair was still wet and his shirt was clinging to his damp skin. It briefly occurred to her that they would've been showering at the same time, but she had to push that thought far from her mind before any X-rated images had time to form. She was supposed to be regaining control over her urges, not developing more.

'They just want some tales of life in the real world so they can gasp with horror and thank their bank balance it's not them.' He always sounded so cynical when he talked about his family, and though she understood why she wished he could reconcile his way of life with theirs. For his own sake.

He would only twist himself in knots trying to make them into people they weren't. She should know. Growing up she thought she had the perfect family, the idyllic upbringing. Finding out that she'd been adopted had changed everything. Her parents became strangers to her, who'd lied about who she was her entire life. She wished she could go back in time and have the relationship with them she'd once had, at least then she wouldn't feel as alone as she did now.

Though she'd understood when they explained they'd kept her real parentage a secret because they didn't want to cause her any pain, their relationship had been altered for ever.

And then Steve had upended her life. At a time when she needed to feel some security, she'd begun the search to trace her birth family. Already fragile and feeling betrayed, that devastating news of their deaths had brought all of that resentment back to the fore. Everyone close to her had let her down. First Steve, taking everything, then her parents, denying her that closure with her birth family. She'd felt completely adrift ever since, not knowing who she really was, or who she was supposed to have been. It seemed every time she figured that out, her identity was ripped away from her. If she wasn't Steve's future wife, or Jo Kirkham, then who was she?

After the break-up she should've been able to lean on her parents, cry on her mum's shoulder and revert to a child in need of comfort. Except that new layer of betrayal, that feeling that her parents were responsible for keeping her from making that important connection with her birth family, seemed to destroy what was left of their relationship. She'd only gone back home to stay with them out of necessity, and everyone knew it. Now they tiptoed around each other, leading their own lives. It was sad really and she wished they could find some sort of resolution, but she didn't know how. They probably needed a good talk to clear the air and for her to air her grievances, but she didn't want to rock the boat when they were providing her with a roof over her head.

She didn't even have any friends to turn to any more. Most of them disappeared with her ex. Either embarrassed by her change in circumstances or not wanting to get drawn into any drama. So she'd effectively been on her own since, fighting her way back. Probably for the best when she found it so difficult to let anyone get close these days. It seemed the only way to keep herself protected. Opening up her world to anyone now just seemed like inviting trouble, giving them carte blanche to mess with her heart.

Although Taylor didn't have her money worries, his life seemed pretty solitary too. Only around his family when he had to be. She hoped some day they could all find a way to live in harmony when it wasn't an ideal situation for anyone.

'How do you deal with that?' Unlike her, Taylor didn't strike her as someone who would bite his tongue or put on a show to keep anyone happy.

He shrugged. 'They know how I feel. I tell them often enough. I just hope someday I can get through to them and that they'll make an effort too. We're just very different people. I've come to realise that now, after spending half my life wondering why my mother and I weren't good enough for my dad. Why he needed to replace us.'

'I'm sure it's not like that at all. You know, my parents kept the information that I was adopted from me, until I discovered the truth at eighteen. It changed our relationship for ever when I found out my birth parents had died without me ever meeting them. Please don't let anything stop you from being with your family. One day it'll be too late to change anything.'

'I know that was upsetting for you, Jo, but couldn't you forgive your parents too? Perhaps they were simply trying to protect you. That's how much they love you.' Taylor's outside view of her situation was simplistic at best, but Jo realised it was also true.

She'd been so caught up in anger and grief these past two years she'd neglected the reasons why her parents had been so afraid of telling her the truth. It had been easy to put the blame on them being selfish. Ironically, it had taken her telling Taylor to hold on to his family at any cost, for her to realise she didn't want to lose the one she had. That they had been acting out of fear, and love for her. They still needed to have that big talk, but perhaps she could cut them some slack and try to salvage her relationship with them. After all, it was the only one she had in her life now. Another reason Taylor should keep trying with his family when he was as closed off to other people as she was, and might need his loved ones around him some day too.

'I'll talk to them when I get home. I promise. What about your family? What would it take for you to feel closer to them?'

His heavy sigh told of his frustration at the situation more than his words ever would. As though he didn't expect it to ever happen, and he knew he was fighting a losing battle. 'Anything. Just have some awareness of the world beyond their cosy bubble. Dad's always about the next big product, the "must have" that becomes another source of income to fund his next project. I'm sure he makes charity donations, probably for tax purposes, but I'd like him to give something back that came from the heart.'

'Like setting up a mobile clinic.' She couldn't help but smile knowing that was the kind of person Taylor was. A man with a heart, and a conscience as big as his bank balance.

'Yeah.' He gave her a lopsided smile that made her tummy flutter with nervy butterflies. 'Or a whole hospital. He can afford it.'

By now they'd reached the beach bar, which went way beyond the title and the picture she'd had in her mind of a grass hut serving drinks. The bar itself, although it did have some sort of thatch and bamboo roof, was as big as she'd ever seen. She imagined with more than the one member of staff currently mixing drinks behind the counter they could serve hundreds if the Strouds ever decided to throw a festival of some sort.

There were huge daybeds arranged into a sort of cul-de-sac. They were so close together she wondered if this arrangement was specially for this afternoon. She imagined on a normal day they'd be spread out to afford people more privacy and a better view of the ocean. This set-up seemed more in keeping with the 'story time' vibe Taylor had suggested they'd planned.

The rest of the family and his siblings' partners were already spread out on the luxury seating awaiting their arrival. Unfortunately, that meant Jo and Taylor had been left to share one of the bed areas.

'Glad to see you made it back in one piece, bro.' Taylor's stepbrother, whom she recognised from back home, reached up from his prone position to high-five him.

'You too, Jo. I'm sure it can't have been easy being stranded there last night. I would've been terrified.' The youngest of the Stroud offspring, Allegra, fanned herself in horror at the thought.

Jo had to do her best not to laugh. Taylor's predictions of his family's reactions had been pretty spot on.

'It wasn't too bad. The local community really made us feel welcome, made sure we had plenty to eat and were comfortable for the night.' Even the mention of their night together made her think about their passionate embrace and sent her temperature rising.

'Sit down, sit down. Tell us everything.' Taylor's father headed back from the bar carrying a cocktail, followed by several staff who distributed similar colourful concoctions to the rest of the party.

Jo accepted the sunset-coloured drink garnished with gaudy paper decorations and streamers, then tried to manoeuvre herself onto the thin mattress-like cushion without spilling it. Something told her the cream-coloured upholstery wouldn't survive it. She shuffled back and tried to keep herself propped upright on the many oversized cushions that were lying around. When Taylor came to join her, the bed dipped in the middle, causing them to roll closer to each other, but she couldn't scrabble away without making it obvious she was affected by him and had to remain where she was. For somewhere designed to be the ultimate luxury chill-out area she wasn't comfortable in the slightest.

With everyone sitting listening in anticipation she knew the onus was on them to make conversation.

'Well, we set up a clinic in the local community centre. A man called Isaac made the arrangements and before long we had a queue of people waiting to see us. All bringing us gifts.' She showed off the seashell necklace she was wearing.

'You have to understand these people have to get a boat or a plane over to the mainland just to get seen to,' Taylor interjected. 'That's if they can afford to do so, and if there's transport available. A pop-up clinic like the one we provided won't make any difference long-term, but we advised and treated as many people as we could. Having Jo there meant I could see twice as many people since she was able to see to a lot of the minor injuries and queries for me.' Taylor joined in her account to point out the necessity of the work he did, not, she suspected for praise, but in an attempt to garner them into action themselves.

'That's very commendable of you, Jo.' Though Mr Stroud's comment was probably well meant, it made her wince at his lack of tact. Not only had he missed the point, but he'd neglected to acknowledge his son's incredible contribution. He was the architect of the whole thing after all.

She was beginning to see where Taylor's frustration with his family came from.

'What happens in emergencies?' his stepsister asked, pulling her feet up on her bed until she was almost in the foetal position.

'Well, they have to try to get them to the mainland where the hospital is, but failing that, they have to deal with the problem themselves. You can see the issue…in these remote areas the mortality rate is a lot higher than the cities that have accessible medical help.' Again, Taylor tried to reiterate why investment of time and money was so important in the work that he did.

'We actually had an emergency when we were there yesterday. A young boy had an accident, and his body was peppered with shards of glass. As we were removing them, Taylor found one embedded very close to his spine. I dread to think what would have happened if he hadn't been able to successfully remove it.' Jo thought it was equally important for Taylor's family to recognise the difference he personally was making in this quest.

'Really?' It was Taylor's stepmother, Victoria, who voiced her surprise at this snippet of information. As though she wasn't aware of her stepson's abilities, and they'd been under the impression his medical qualifications had been little more than a hobby. That they'd been indulging his ventures abroad in the same fashion as his siblings' interests in racing cars or running a fashion line.

Jo turned to look at Taylor, silently questioning why he hadn't told them in detail about the work he did. He avoided eye contact with her, instead getting up to help himself to some of the snacks that had been laid out on the glass-topped rattan table set up in the middle of their little commune.

'Yes. Taylor's so much more than a doctor. He's an emergency service in his own right.' She didn't miss the smirk on Taylor's face even if he didn't rise to the bait.

'I don't know how you do it.' His stepsister fanned herself again, and Jo marvelled in the difference between the siblings. She admired Taylor even more for going out on his own when he could easily have led this pampered lifestyle safe from the horrors of the real world.

'I think you deserve something to eat after all of that.' Mr Stroud senior got to his feet and helped his wife up with him. She was wearing a cloud of chiffon and seemed to glide towards the bar area that had been laid out with silver platters full of barbecued delights.

With no signs, nor smell, of the food cooking, Jo had to assume it had been barbecued elsewhere so the smoke wouldn't offend the hosts. A contrast to the dinner she'd shared with Taylor last night, which they'd eaten out of tinfoil parcels with their hands. Perhaps he'd been adopted too…

Whilst everyone headed up to the bar, Jo headed straight for Taylor. 'Why don't you tell them what you do? You're amazing and they should know it.'

He gave her a sad sort of smile. An acceptance of the situation even though it was obviously unfair. 'It's not about me, is it?'

Jo acted on impulse then, throwing her arms

around his neck to hug him, and offer a little comfort. Forgetting the no touching rule she was supposed to have in place. He rested his head momentarily on her shoulder, his arms slipping around her waist, as he gave a small sigh. Then he let go and joined the others at the buffet laid out—the reason they were here.

She took a moment to compose herself before following him over to the bar area. The moment surprising her in all sorts of ways. Not only had her reaction been unexpected, but so had his. Taylor had leaned into that hug like he really needed it. She knew how it felt to be among family and still feel alone. For the duration of that brief embrace they'd been kindred spirits, and her heart ached for both of them.

'Have you heard anything about your mother's progress?' she asked Mr Stroud, making small talk as they mingled with their plates of food.

'Yes, I checked in with the hospital this morning. They're hoping she can be discharged in a day or two. Hopefully she'll be back for the New Year's Eve party.'

Jo stopped herself from suggesting that it might be more advantageous for the lady's health to go back home and rest, knowing it wasn't her place to do so. If the hospital had said she could still participate in the festivities Jo doubted Isabelle would be put off either. It certainly seemed important to her son that everyone should be here for the party.

'I'm so glad. I was worried about her.' Selfishly, having her charge back meant Jo would be busy again, and less likely to stray back into temptation in the form of her gorgeous grandson.

So he's gorgeous now, huh? that smug little devil on her shoulder who wouldn't be silenced whispered into her ear. Reminding her that the attraction wasn't simply going to disappear because Isabelle was coming back.

'The doctors at the hospital have been wonderful,' he gushed, seemingly oblivious to his own son's achievements.

'You know Taylor provides an extremely valuable service to these communities. He was amazing out there yesterday. You know you should think about going with him some time to see for yourself.' Jo hoped she'd given him some food for thought, but at the same time hoped she still had a job when they got back home.

Once she'd made some excruciating small talk with everyone, she managed to slink back to the daybeds unnoticed. As soon as an acceptable amount of time had passed, she'd excuse herself and go back to the villa. She kicked off her sandals and climbed onto the Taylor-free mattress, which was surprisingly comfy when she wasn't sweating over being in such esteemed company.

With her head on the cushions, she didn't think it would hurt to close her eyes for a while. After all she hadn't had much sleep last night. Jo drifted off with the sound of the sea and the white noise of the other guests chatting playing her a lullaby.

'Jo.'

Even though Jo knew Taylor running hand in hand with her along the shore was a dream, it seemed so real. She couldn't wipe the grin off her face, and she swore she could even hear his voice.

'Jo.'

It was getting louder now, and for some reason he was shaking her by the arm.

'Everyone's gone back to the house. I don't want to leave you out here all night.' Taylor's voice sounded as though it was right in her ear now.

Another shake, and the romantic beach stroll began to fade away. Consciousness loomed until she was blinking back into reality and staring into Taylor's velvety brown eyes. He was kneeling next to the daybed, his hand on her arm, apparently trying to get her to wake up.

'Hello, sleepy-head.'

'Hello.' She gave him a lazy smile. He really was a pretty picture to wake up to.

'We didn't want to wake you up when you were sleeping so soundly, but everyone's gone back to the villa and I told the staff they could finish for the day. I didn't want to leave you here on your own.'

Fully awake now, embarrassment flooding every cell in her body, Jo sat up. 'I'm so sorry. That must've seemed so rude after all the trouble they'd gone to.'

'It's fine. They knew we were both exhausted, and let's face it, it was the staff who did all this.' Taylor definitely had a lovely bedside manner, capable of putting her immediately at ease with his humour.

The fairy lights that she hadn't noticed strung up around the canopies suddenly came on as the natural light began to fade. It was magical.

'This is so beautiful.' She lay back down again to appreciate the view.

To her surprise, Taylor climbed up onto the bed and lay down beside her. 'I guess it is. Stuff like this I take for granted.'

'Well, I think you've proved you don't need it. Still, it's a nice change from a freezing cold community hall.' Though they were effectively tucked up in bed together again.

'I don't know, it had its charms…' He turned to look at her, and Jo's heart gave a happy sigh.

'It's been a weird couple of days, hasn't it?' She tried to change the subject, afraid of what would happen if they lingered on last night's events. Despite the open air and the sea breeze around them, the air seemed thick with tension. Anticipation of what tonight would bring.

'You're telling me.' Taylor released her from his hypnotic gaze, flopping onto his back to stare up at the night sky and the stars beginning to wink at them from above. 'Dad told me he was proud of me. Then he literally patted me on the back.'

He seemed genuinely taken aback by the praise. Whilst Jo was pleased for him, it also shouldn't be such a big deal for his father to acknowledge he was doing something worthwhile. Of course, Taylor didn't need anyone to validate him. He knew what he was doing was incredibly important. But like everyone, deep down, she suspected he craved his family's approval. It would ruin the moment if she told him it was likely her who'd prompted his father's unexpected display. He didn't need to know that, and it would likely embarrass him to find out she'd been canvassing on his behalf. Besides, they'd see his brilliance for themselves eventually. It had only taken her a matter of hours to realise what an amazing person he was.

'It's about time. Next thing you know he'll be funding a new hospital wing in your name.'

Taylor narrowed his eyes at her. 'Let's not get too carried away. I'll settle for him realising I'm not just playing doctor.'

'Well, you're definitely not doing that any more than I'm playing nurse.' It wasn't meant as anything more than a throwaway comment. Yet the way he was looking at her suggested it had been so much more. As though she'd suggested playing doctors and nurses together.

The atmosphere seemed to change between them then. The darkness prettified by the fairy lights, and the gentle swish of the waves on the shore only increasing the romance of the moment as they lay together.

'You do wonders for my self-esteem, you know that?'

'I wouldn't have thought you needed any help in that department. You always seem so sure of yourself.'

'It's all an act. More like self-preservation than anything else. If I exude confidence, then no one else can take advantage of me. Or something like that…'

An overwhelming surge of something seemed to wash over Jo as he opened up to her. That vulnerability making all her defences melt away too. Because she recognised it. That need to put on an act, to hide the hurt and just keep on going. She didn't have to imagine what his ex had put him through, because she'd felt it too. The betrayal, the thought of never trusting anyone again, and the loss not only of the relationship, but also the person you'd once been. It was devastating. His heart was as broken as hers.

'I can understand that… I haven't been able to forgive my parents for keeping my adoption secret, and it will take a lot for me to trust anyone again. When Steve came along, I let him into my life—'

'And he betrayed you all over again. I'm so sorry, Jo, but you're not the one to blame here. If anything, you're the victim. You shouldn't be punishing yourself for something he did when you still have a life to live. Don't shut yourself off from the world.'

'Says you. Isn't that exactly what you're doing too, Taylor? Flitting from one place to another, never staying long enough to get close to anyone so they don't hurt you the way Imogen did. You were the victim there too. You deserve happiness as much as I do.'

'And what? That means leaving myself open to someone else who wants to steal and lie their way into my heart?'

'I'm just saying that it might be nice to share the life you have with someone. You don't have to be alone.'

He sighed. 'I've made my peace with the life I have, but you seem stuck somewhere that's making you unhappy. You deserve so much more, Jo.' Taylor put an arm around her and pulled her close.

'We both do.' She leaned into him, and the moment seemed reminiscent of last night. Only this time she wasn't in search of warmth. At least not in the purely physical meaning. Right now, she felt as though she'd found someone with whom she shared a connection, but didn't have to fear. They both knew how it felt to be betrayed, and neither of them was ready to open up fully to the idea of another relationship. That didn't mean they couldn't explore the intimacy that usually came as part of the deal. For two years she'd been avoiding the idea of being with another man because she didn't want her feelings hurt. Perhaps with Taylor she could finally relax and enjoy the physical closeness he offered without having to keep herself protected at all times. Because Taylor would be out of her life again as quickly as he'd entered it.

When the kiss came, it felt like the most natural thing in the world. There were no alarm bells ringing, or red lights flashing, because she wanted it. She needed the comfort, the romance and the passion she'd already tasted on his lips.

This time they started slow, letting that fire burn steadily between them. She hadn't realised how much she'd missed the intimacy of a simple kiss until Taylor had first pressed his lips against hers. That feeling of letting go, of giving herself completely, physically and emotionally in that moment came as a relief. She could feel his hands on her waist through the thin fabric of her dress, branding her, claiming her as his. The thought of which made her tremble; arousal and anticipation coursing through her body.

His mouth was crushing hers now, his tongue flicking tantalisingly against hers, that fire spreading, raging out of control. She was burning everywhere he touched her, and places where she wanted him to touch her. Aching, craving, needing Taylor. Only Taylor.

'What if someone sees us?' Her voice was breathy, heavy with desire and excitement. She wanted this, but she was an employee of his father's, and certainly not an exhibitionist.

'I'm on it.' Taylor jumped up and unfurled the canopies on all sides, so they fell down creating a curtain all around them. Ensconcing them in their own private room on the beach.

'Very nifty,' she said watching him work.

'I have my uses.' His eyes twinkled with the promise of more, making her tingle all over at the thought of him working more of his magic on her.

This was her moment to change her mind if she wanted to. When she was able to think clearly without Taylor touching her, kissing her, and rendering her a slave to her libido. She didn't need the lifeline because she wasn't going anywhere. Especially not now that Taylor was pulling off his shirt, exposing that hard body she couldn't resist reaching out to stroke. His shaky intake of breath when she touched him was reassuring. This wasn't the norm for him either.

They'd both been wounded by their exes. Afraid to trust or get close to anyone again. She wondered, if like her, he'd been too hurt to share a bed with anyone since. Not only did it give them a deeper connection, but it also made her feel more relaxed that she wasn't the only one out of her comfort zone. Based on a kiss alone she didn't think they'd have a problem with compatibility, but there was always the worry that she would be found lacking in some way. Especially when it had been so long since she'd been intimate with anyone.

Then Taylor was kissing her again and all of her anxiety melted away.

He slipped the straps of her dress over her shoulders, sliding his hands over her skin and raising goose bumps in his wake. With greedy palms, he pushed her strapless bra down and cupped her breasts. Jo gasped at the strong grip, sighed as he brushed his thumbs over her nipples, turned to liquid when he pinched them between his fingers. It didn't matter that they were in the lap of luxury on a private island, she knew he could make her feel this way wherever they were.

Taylor's trousers were already riding low on his hips, and they didn't take much coaxing from an eager Jo to slide on down past his backside along with his boxers. He kicked them off so he was gloriously naked, prompting her to strip off the rest of her clothes too. She lay beneath him, her breath coming in short, shallow gasps. This was her at her most vulnerable. She was trusting Taylor with her heart, her body and her peace of mind. When he paused to look at her, she held her breath, hoping that he wasn't going to find her wanting in any way. If he rejected her now she didn't think she'd ever be able to trust again.

'You're beautiful,' he finally said, letting her breathe again.

His ever-darkening eyes and hardening body led her to believe he was being genuine. It did wonders for her confidence, giving her the bravado to reach for him. To stroke the epitome of his masculinity. He closed his eyes and his intake of breath soon exhaled on a sigh as she moved her hand along his rock-hard shaft. The sense of power she felt, at a time when circumstances had been out of her control for so long, was an aphrodisiac all of its own. Not that she needed one when this gorgeous man was naked and…*oh*… Now he was flicking his tongue over her nipples, sucking almost until that point of pain. The balance of power had definitely tipped in his favour again.

They seemed determined to drive one another to the brink of madness, touching, teasing, tasting one another's bodies. Mouths clashing, hands exploring, she was molten at her core; ready for him.

'What about contraception?' she asked, barely clinging to the last atom of common sense in her body.

Taylor swore, as though in the heat of their passion he'd forgotten too. It was easily done when they were so engrossed in one another; so close to that relief and release they were searching for.

He only left her for a moment to retrieve his wallet from his trousers, rummaging with shaking fingers for that little foil packet. Jo waited impatiently as he sheathed himself, kissing his neck and nibbling on his earlobe until he was groaning with frustration. She liked that she could drive him wild. That she could make him feel the way she did.

He pushed her back down onto the bed, kissed her all over until she was writhing and wanton beneath him, desperate to make that last connection.

When Taylor joined his body with hers, she clutched him tight, trying to stay grounded when she was already soaring.

'You feel so good.' Jo could hear the restraint in his voice as he kissed her, made sure she was comfortable, relaxed, before taking things to the next level.

It was tempting to race ahead, to get to that finish line as soon as possible, but she suspected they both needed much more than that final release. They needed the intimacy, the comfort to be had in sharing their bodies with one another. The ultimate test of trust.

CHAPTER SEVEN

TAYLOR TOOK HIS TIME, moving slowly at first. Giving them both the opportunity to adjust to one another, to revel in the sensation. She felt like heaven. So soft and warm around him he knew he'd never want to leave.

Neither of them had planned this, but from the moment he'd kissed her it had seemed inevitable. That level of passion wasn't something found every day, and clearly couldn't be contained. There was a chemistry between them they hadn't been able to ignore, and now would be impossible to forget. Especially now he knew she didn't want anything serious.

She'd thrown his own words back at him. Made him think about how he'd been a victim too, had been punishing himself. Denying any chance he'd had to find happiness in anything other than his work. Although he still wasn't ready to jump into a relationship, and might never be, seeing his situation in a different light gave him permission to enjoy this moment with Jo. To totally let himself go just for a little while.

Jo squeezed her inner muscles around him and short-circuited his brain so he couldn't think straight, only feel. And he wanted more. She was raking his skin with her nails, wrapping her legs around him to draw him in deeper, urging him not to hold back. Driven by lust he picked up the pace, every thrust of his hips bringing him closer to the edge. He didn't want to get there before Jo.

With one hand, he cupped her breast, her pert nipple too tantalising to resist. He sucked hard, causing her to buck against him with a gasp. Whilst teasing the pink tip with his teeth and tongue, he reached down between their bodies and pressed his thumb into her soft mound. Her gasp spurred him on, thrusting, teasing, sucking, until they were both slick with her arousal.

When her orgasm hit, she muffled her cry in the crook of his neck, rocking with him until her body was limp. Taylor's restraint broke, and a primal roar ripped from him as he gave into that final bliss. He climaxed so hard and fast he felt as though he was giving her a piece of his soul.

In a way, he was. Jo was the only person he'd let down his defences with since Imogen. Not only had he shared his passion project with her, and details of his personal life, but now he'd shared his body too; he'd given her everything he could.

And it still wasn't enough. Because deep down he was still wary, of everyone capable of hurting him. That meant holding back.

As wonderful as Jo was, he wasn't able to take that final leap into a relationship. Not that she wanted that either. She'd made it clear she wasn't ready for a serious commitment. Perhaps that was why he'd given into temptation, because he knew she wasn't expecting more than he was willing to give. He didn't know if he could ever trust anyone, including himself, not to break his heart, or his trust again.

He lay down beside her, his heart thumping, and his chest heaving as he recovered from his exertions.

'That was amazing.' Jo practically purred as she curled her body around him and pulled the decorative throw up over their bodies. He suspected the move was more about covering her nudity, making her feel less exposed, than the need for warmth. Despite the cool night air, their bodies were slick with sweat.

'I didn't even use all my best moves.'

'Oh? Are you saving them for next time?' she asked, batting her eyelashes, attempting a casualness that didn't quite work because of the hitch in her voice.

Jo was asking if this was a one-time deal and he didn't know how to answer that without spoiling the mood. He didn't want to upset her, but he also had to be realistic. It wouldn't be fair to lead her on when he still wasn't in the right head space for a relationship. Not to mention their different lifestyles, which wouldn't be conducive to anything long-term even if he was to consider it.

'Listen, Jo…'

'Such a serious face.' She mocked him with a scowl and pursed lips to make him smile and feel even worse.

Taylor sighed. 'This was great, but I, uh, I don't know where I'm going to be from one month to the next. I can't commit to anything.'

'I didn't ask you to.'

'You know what I mean… I'd like to do this again. Preferably somewhere more private. Where I have all night to show you my moves.' There would have to be something seriously wrong with him not to want to do this again, but he wouldn't risk anyone getting hurt in the process.

'I'm curious to find out what else you have in your locker, Taylor, when you've already surpassed yourself. That doesn't mean I'm looking for anything beyond that. We can keep things casual. Believe me, I've enough going on in my life without the hassle of another relationship. I'm still recovering from the last one. As, I suspect, are you.'

'You want to do this again? Just sex?' It was

a tempting idea, and would mean he could have Jo in his life for a little while longer. Without the worry that she was going to break his heart.

'Why not? No promises, no commitment. Just company, and great sex. Sounds ideal to me. I think it'll help both of us move on from the past.' When she put it that way, Taylor didn't see any problem, other than having to get used to an empty bed again once it was all over.

There was just something about the arrangement that seemed a little…off. Clinical even. It was obvious they were both holding back from committing to anything because of their past relationship issues, but things got messy when emotions got involved. Painful. Perhaps this was the ideal solution. At least for now.

'I suppose we could keep seeing one another for the duration of this trip. Then, once the New Year comes, we'll go our separate ways with some very nice memories to take with us.' It meant he wasn't even committing to anything beyond these few days together. By setting a time limit, there was no risk of things getting complicated. New Year's was their deadline, and it would be nice to start afresh once he left the island.

'What about your father?'

'I'm not into threesomes. Especially not with close family members.'

Jo rolled her eyes at him. 'I think one Stroud

man is more than enough for me to handle, thank you. I meant that I'm technically an employee. I'm here to look after his mother. Not for a romantic getaway.'

Taylor traced a fingertip over her décolletage and was rewarded when she bit her lip. It was clear once wasn't going to be enough for either of them.

'I don't see why you can't do both. No one else has to know. We have a day or two before my grandmother comes back anyway.'

'You mean sneak around?'

'We can be stealthy, yes. Sex ninjas.' In one quick motion he pulled the cover up over their heads, making Jo squeal with surprise.

'I like the sound of that,' she said as they were cocooned in their own little blanket bubble, her eyes twinkling in the semi darkness. He wished they were on their own, on a mini break together, free to explore the island without fear of incurring his father's wrath.

They both knew he wouldn't approve. Not least because of the nature of their agreement to keep things purely about sex. It was definitely no one else's business. He didn't want what they had together to be reduced to something shameful. Then he could leave what had happened between them here and move on without regret or recriminations. He didn't want Jo to lose her job either. She had a life to go back to, and she obviously needed the money to help her get back on her feet.

He wished so many things were different.

The only way he knew how to make reality disappear was to lose himself in Jo. He kissed her again, and with their naked bodies pressed tightly together it wasn't long before his attentions were focused elsewhere.

'Why don't we take this back to the house?' At least then they'd have some privacy and there was the chance of spending the night together. He couldn't remember the last time he'd woken up next to someone in bed. The closest he'd come was kipping down with other medical professionals who'd volunteered their time on similar outreach programmes with him. It wasn't quite the same. On those occasions he'd usually spent the night trying not to touch whoever happened to be sharing a hostel or a tent with him. He wasn't always guaranteed a bed, never mind the luxury of his father's villa.

'Like this?' Jo gestured to her naked form, giving him an excuse to drink in the sight of her again. 'I'm not sure I want to be caught streaking across the beach, thanks.'

'Now, there's an idea.' He could just picture her running across the sand under the moonlight carefree into his arms.

'What?' She eyed him cautiously.

'Skinny dipping. When was the last time you did that?'

'Uh, never.'

'You don't know what you're missing. We used to do it all the time as medical students when we went on trips to the beach. There's something very liberating about stripping off outside in the night air. As though you're casting off all of your problems, even for a few minutes.'

'Sounds like heaven.' She sighed, as though she had the weight of the world on her shoulders. Taylor wanted her to forget everything bringing her down for as long as possible. There would be time enough for reality to crowd them and bring them back down to earth from their post-sex high.

'So you're in?' He was seizing on the slight waiver in her first refusal to even entertain the idea.

'I'd be mortified if anyone saw me.' It wasn't a flat-out no.

'No one will come down this way now when they have everything they need back at the villa. I'll take a look and make sure there's no one around. We'll see if anyone's coming down and can make a run for the sea if needs be.'

She didn't look convinced, but Taylor decided to take the initiative anyway and ducked outside. He walked around the bar and a little bit along the shore, looking out for any signs of life.

It was as invigorating being naked in the open air as he'd remembered. Hopefully, he'd be able to convince Jo to join him. As well as thinking it would be good for her to let loose for a while, he knew it was another memory he'd have to cherish for the rest of his days. Much preferable to the times he'd larked around with uni mates dunking each other under the water and generally messing about. Back in the days when he'd been oblivious to anyone else's needs but his own.

'The coast is clear,' he said, sticking his head around the curtain of the bed.

'I'm not sure about this…' She was hesitant, but she did get up, their blanket wrapped around her body for now.

'Come on…live a little.' He held out his hand to take hers and led her out into the open.

She looked furtively around and seemed to relax when she was convinced there was no one else lurking nearby. Taylor waggled his eyebrows suggestively at her and watched with a grin as she dropped the blanket and revealed herself to him.

'Aah!' She let out a shriek, grabbed his hand and ran down towards the sea.

'The water's freezing!' Her eyes were sparkling in the darkness, wide and full of the thrill of the moment.

He felt it too.

'But it feels great. Right?' They waded out until

the water was up to their shoulders, their naked-
ness hidden from sight should anyone venture out
on a late-night walk along the shore.

'I'll tell you when I get my breath back.'

'I'm proud of you for doing this.' He meant it.
Even though the water was cold, and he couldn't
feel anything from the neck down, he was glad
they were doing this and being silly together. It
made a change from the serious life-or-death work
he did every day, and he'd forgotten what it was
just to have fun for the sake of it. He suspected it
was the same for Jo after everything she'd been
dealing with recently.

'So am I. I never thought I'd do anything like
this. It is kind of freeing. Maybe I'll become a
naturist.' Jo seemed to be in her element. She
jumped up out of the water giving him a flash of
her beautiful round breasts before splashing the
water around him soaking them both.

'Maybe we should find our own deserted island and just live off the land, like a regular pair
of castaways.' He moved towards her, suddenly
feeling the urge to have her in his arms again.

'I wish.' She slicked her wet hair back with both
hands, looking like some sort of water nymph, be-
witching him and liable to drag him to a watery
death, but he didn't care. He'd die a happy death
with a naked Jo coiled around his body.

'You're beautiful.' The words slipped out of his mouth unbidden, but true.

He kissed her. Not caring about the cold noses or other frozen body parts. He cupped her backside and held her flush against him, wishing he'd taken his own advice and gone back to the warmth and comfort of the villa in the first place.

'Let's go before we end up with hypothermia,' Jo said eventually, reading his mind and taking him by the hand.

They walked back to the daybeds, his arm around her, as though strolling around naked was commonplace for both of them, and there was no one else in this world. It didn't take them long to pull their clothes on again, both eager to get back to the house as soon as possible.

Jo didn't know what had come over her. She was like a different woman since she'd met Taylor. These past two years she'd been nothing but cautious. Hurt and feeling guilty about the other people who'd been affected by her ex's betrayal, her life had become a struggle for survival and trying to clear up the damage he'd left in his wake. Not to mention the devastation caused by the news that her birth parents had died without her ever getting to know them, finding out that part of her was now lost for ever.

Taylor had reminded her who she was. Not only

was she someone who could make a difference in other people's lives, but she was also a woman with a lot of life to live. She'd enjoyed working with him, getting to know the man he was, but she'd also loved the person she was with him. A young woman having fun. She'd only been able to do that because she trusted him. It was a risky strategy, but so far it seemed to be working.

Now as they made their way back to the villa, bodies still wet and smelling of the ocean, it was as thrilling as running on the shore naked. Equally as exhilarating because she knew what was waiting for her beyond the bedroom door already.

Taylor was keen for them to have some privacy so he could show her his 'best moves'. Judging by the time they'd already spent together she knew she was in for something special. She only hoped they wouldn't wake the rest of the house with their antics or else they'd have some serious explaining to do.

When Mr Stroud senior had asked her to come on this trip for his mother's sake, so she could enjoy the New Year celebrations with the rest of the family, Jo would never have believed this was where she'd end up. Nor that she would have agreed to a casual sex arrangement with his son. It seemed an ideal set-up for two people who were afraid to commit in case they got hurt. She just prayed it stayed that way. Sharing her life with someone in any capacity again was a risk, and if it backfired on her she doubted she'd trust anyone ever again. As long as she kept their New Year's end date in mind, hopefully there wouldn't be any emotional fallout.

'Are you okay, gorgeous?' Taylor must have mistaken her introspection for apprehension, but there was absolutely no need. She'd never been as sure about anything as she was about spending the night with him. Sleeping with him had been the only bit of happiness she'd had in over two years, and getting the chance to do it again was a no-brainer. Who wouldn't want to be ravished by a handsome doctor, worshipped and brought to the point of orgasm again and again?

'I'm fine. I just don't want to get caught sneaking into your room.' That was the one thing she was wary of, apart from having her heart and her trust broken all over again. She didn't want to lose her job, as well. She couldn't afford to.

'We'll be as quiet as church mice. At least until we get to my room.' He gave her a wink that suggested reasons for them to be making a lot of noise. All of which made her tremble more with the anticipation of his promises.

When they reached the front door, he put his finger on his lips. They were giggling like naughty teenagers about to be busted sneaking in from a party they'd been told they weren't allowed to attend. Hand in hand they tiptoed down the quiet hallways to his room. Once they were inside, the door closed, locking them away in their own world again, they let passion flare to life again. Kissing and tearing each other's clothes off like they'd been denied each other a lifetime, rather than a few minutes.

She hoped it would be like this every time they got together. It would give her something to look forward to, as well as something to cling to when she was back to her lonely life. For two years she'd been consumed by work and trying to earn a living. There hadn't been any real joy in her life since everything had fallen apart. Neither her work life, nor her home life, were making her particularly happy. Perhaps this was the start of things beginning to turn around.

Once she had enough money saved for a deposit, she'd move into her own place. A picture flashed into her mind of what that would be like as it so often did. Maybe she might eventually be able to travel. This trip had given her a taste for that. Except when she thought about travelling somewhere hot and sultry, Taylor inevitably became part of the scene, lying in bed next to her. She shook off the romantic fantasy, a little perturbed by those thoughts creeping in uninvited. It was a dream that went too far and she needed to rid herself of the notion that this was anything other than a short fling. It was enough for now. A step forward without rushing in too fast into a new relationship.

They tumbled into bed, keen to pick up where they'd left off. Rolling around atop the mattress in a tangle of limbs and naked bodies, clinging to one another as though their lives depended on it. In that moment, he felt like Jo's whole world. Nothing else mattered except his kisses, his touch and the things he was doing to her. Taylor made her feel alive for the first time in years. Before then she'd been nothing more than an automaton simply going through the motions. Wake, work, sleep, repeat.

Now she was a real girl. A woman who had feelings, wants and needs, that were apparently all wrapped up in Taylor. He already knew how to make her happy, to satisfy her and to make her moan in ecstasy.

This must be one of his moves he'd boasted about...

Lying back, with Taylor appreciating every inch of her body with his mouth and his tongue, Jo had never felt so wanted. Even when she'd been with Steve, she didn't remember being so relaxed and turned on at the same time. Probably because there had always been a difference in the balance of power between them, with him always in control.

In hindsight, she'd worshipped him too much, never seeing any wrong in him. Oblivious to his faults until it was too late.

Perhaps in her desperate search for stability she'd clung to the idea of him, and who they could be together. Hopefully a family someday. He'd used that belief in him to his advantage, swindling her out of her business as well as that dream. She'd handed him too much of her power, deferred to him when it came to the business as a way of showing him how much she loved him. It was different with Taylor. When they worked together it had felt like sharing the load equally. A mutual respect and understanding of each other's roles. That hadn't been the case with her ex who'd always treated her as his inferior despite the fact it had been her business. He'd joined her later as a partner after they'd started going out together. When she'd signed over half of her business, she hadn't realised her life as she knew it would never be the same. And not in a good way.

Only now was she beginning to be optimistic about the future, and Taylor had been a part of that by making her feel so good. She hadn't thought another man, or great sex, would be part of her life, but she could see now what she'd been missing out on. With any luck her life now on would be full on every level and the euphoria wouldn't begin and end on this island.

Taylor was teasing her intimately with his tongue, dipping in and out, bringing her to the edge over and over. Until she was begging him to help her reach that final release. Only then did he retrieve a condom from his nightstand and give her what she was craving.

He filled her, drove deep inside her until she felt as though she was flying high above her own body. Then he withdrew from her, bringing her crashing down to earth. Taylor flipped her onto her side, and thrust inside her again from behind, the change of angle causing new sensations, equally arousing. His hands were on her breasts, squeezing, tugging at her nipples, and flooding all of her erogenous zones at once. Hot breath in her ear, lips on the sensitive skin at her neck— this man knew what he was doing. He seemed to anticipate what she needed, and more. Even the sound of his breath getting shallower as he came closer to climax was a turn-on. She rocked back against him, meeting the thrust of his hips with her own, both gasping as they climbed higher and higher. Then he reached between her legs, dipped a finger inside her and stroked until she was completely undone.

She tried to muffle her cry into the pillow so she wouldn't wake the house even though

she wanted to scream her release from the hill-
tops. Taylor followed soon after, his groan sending aftershocks rippling through her body. As if
they'd both ridden out an earthquake and lived
to tell the tale. She supposed in a way they had.
The earth had definitely moved, and she was sure
something else had shifted between them too as
they drifted off to sleep still lying in one another's arms.

CHAPTER EIGHT

'I SUPPOSE WE should make an appearance or it's going to look suspicious if we're both MIA.' Taylor snuggled up behind Jo, showing no sign of getting out of bed.

She knew he was right, but she preferred where she was. It was nice waking up in the morning to a hard male body wrapped around hers making her feel safe and protected. Convincing her that she didn't have to be on her own any more.

It was tempting to pull the covers over their heads again and forget the real reason she was on this island.

The sound of the villa coming alive, footsteps outside as the staff began their working day taking care of the Stroud family, finally roused her. She was supposed to be one of them. Here to work, not lounge around in bed pretending this was her world.

'I'll run the gauntlet back to my room and try and avoid bumping into anyone.' The thought of potentially embarrassing them both and causing upset to the rest of the family brought her back down to earth with a bump.

In an ideal world they wouldn't have to sneak around. And she wouldn't have to think of herself as a second-class citizen. More than that, there wouldn't be a clock ticking down on their time together and they'd see each other whenever they pleased, because they'd both recovered from the scars of their last relationships.

However, the reality was that none of that was possible and she had to be thankful for the snatched time they could have together.

She threw back the covers and retrieved yesterday's clothes from the bedroom floor.

'I'll grab a shower then see you in the kitchen for breakfast. You're welcome to join me for both.' With Taylor striding naked towards the bathroom, it was very tempting, but she didn't want to leave any later before attempting to get back to her own room unseen.

'Maybe next time.' She planted a kiss on his lips on her way out of the door, clearly leaving them both wanting more.

Although her heart was pounding, adrenaline pumping through her veins as she made her way stealthily back to her own room, it wasn't the same as last night. That had been about letting herself go, enjoying the moment with Taylor, and the thrill of it all. This was fear of being discovered and being made to feel ashamed. She didn't want that to ruin what they had.

Once back in her own room she was able to relax. She flicked on the shower, stripped off and stepped into the cubicle. The warm water on her skin reminded her of Taylor's caress, and everywhere he'd touched her. Despite wanting to stay and recall those vivid memories, she was kind of hungry. Jo hadn't eaten much last night and between the late-night swim, and everything else she'd been up to, she'd worked up an appetite.

If she was being truthful, she couldn't wait to see Taylor again. With the circumstances making it difficult for them to be together in the open, she wanted to take any opportunity she had without raising suspicion. Everyone else was going to be at breakfast at some point, so, as long as they could keep their hands off one another, she and Taylor could at least be around each other in company. Anything else would probably have to wait until they were under cover of darkness again.

After rinsing the ocean out of her hair, Jo donned the bikini she'd bought in the hope she would get to see something of the sun. Without Isabelle to look after, or planned work trips with Taylor, perhaps she'd get to lie by the pool for a while after all. That's what everyone else around here seemed to do to fill their days. And, if it meant she got to lust over Taylor in a pair of swim shorts too, it would make their anticipated alone time even hotter than last night.

She pulled on a blue and green cover-up, so she wasn't parading about the villa half naked, and followed the smell of coffee and bacon.

'Good morning.' She breezed into the dining room and tried to hide her disappointment that Taylor wasn't there with his parents.

'Morning, Jo. I hope you didn't sleep outside all night. Taylor promised he'd wake you.' His stepmother poured herself an orange juice, and didn't look the least bit concerned, despite the words coming out of her mouth.

'He did. Thank you.' It was impossible not to think of what else he did for her, which made an awkward atmosphere when she was alone with his parents.

Jo helped herself to some cereal and milk before joining them at the dining table, praying Taylor would make an appearance soon.

'I spoke to the hospital this morning. We're making arrangements to get mother back as soon as possible. She should be back here late afternoon if all goes well.'

'That's great news, Mr Stroud. I'm sure you'll be glad to have her back, as will I.' Regardless that resuming her duties would curtail Jo's time with Taylor, she was looking forward to seeing

Isabelle again, and seeing for herself that she was all right.

'You should make the most of your free time before you have to get back to work,' Mrs Stroud said with a sniff, clearly not impressed that she'd been slacking in her duties despite the circumstances. A reminder that she was merely the hired help. Also, that finding out she was sleeping with Taylor would most certainly warrant instant dismissal.

A sobering thought when she needed every penny she was getting for this trip if she ever hoped to move out from her parents' place.

Then Taylor appeared and she thought it a risk worth taking. He was beautiful. The white T-shirt clinging to his chest emphasised the muscular body she'd explored thoroughly last night, and his wet hair made her think of the offer she'd turned down to join him in the shower. She must have been mad.

'Yes, Jo, you should spend the morning round the pool. I'm sure mother will keep you busy for the rest of this trip.' Taylor's father graciously gave her the go ahead to laze around until her services were required.

'What's this?' Their conversation had clearly caught Taylor's attention as he looked between Jo and his parents.

When his gaze lingered on Jo, she felt her temperature rise. It was going to be difficult not to give away what they'd been up to together when she lit up like a Christmas tree every time he looked at her.

She fought the urge to melt into her chair and attempted a casual response.

'I…er…your father…um…' The more she stuttered, the wider Taylor's grin grew. He tilted his head to one side and waited for her to spit it out.

'We were just telling Jo she's free to use the pool until your grandmother gets back.' Mr Stroud put her out of her misery and answered on her behalf.

'I might do the same. I'm exhausted today for some reason.' The sultry look he shot her was even more devastating to her equilibrium than the grin.

'I think you both deserve some down time. I'm sure you're worn out after your exploits.'

It was all Jo could do not to spit out the mouthful of cereal she'd taken, thanks to his father's well-meaning comment. All she could think about was her 'exploits' with Taylor last night on the beach, and in his bed.

'Definitely. It's really taken a lot out of me.' Taylor wasn't helping, acting as though they were in some bawdy seventies comedy where every other word had a double meaning.

'If you don't mind, I think I'll head out now

whilst it's quiet.' Jo grabbed a piece of toast as she excused herself from the table, hoping to get some time by the pool before the others joined her. It was a bit intimidating being surrounded by the rich and beautiful whose swimwear was more about what they could show off on social media than any practical purpose. She was sure if she tried swimming in one of those cutaway bathing suits she'd end up exposing parts of her body she hadn't meant to.

'That's fine, Jo. As long as you're here for Isabelle when she returns.' Taylor's stepmother dismissed her with another casual reminder of her position.

She didn't let it bother her. It might be different if she was in a proper relationship with Taylor, knowing she would never be good enough for the family, but neither of them wanted that.

Still, as she walked away eating her toast, she bit into it with slightly more aggression than usual.

'Sorry about that.' Taylor jogged after her.

'It's fine. I'm here to look after Isabelle. Your stepmother just likes to remind me of that.'

Taylor winced. 'She forgets she used to actually work for a living too. Sometimes she treats staff as though they're not actually people. That's what's wrong with living in this bubble. There's no concept of the real world, or any self-awareness.'

'It wasn't that long ago you were saying the same sort of thing to me, Taylor.'

This time he looked as though she'd actually punched him in the stomach. 'I guess so. Sorry.'

Taylor appeared so contrite, and with those puppy dog eyes begging her for forgiveness, Jo had no choice but to let it go. After all he'd shown her how much he thought of her since.

'I suppose we're all guilty of making assumptions about one another. That first night I thought you were a rude, entitled, spoilt brat.'

Taylor shrugged. 'Sometimes I am.'

'No, you're not. Now I've got to know you, it's clear you're compassionate, kind and generous.' She didn't need to mention that he was also amazing in bed, when they were both well aware of that fact.

'If you say so…'

'I do.'

'Well, maybe my parents just need to get to know you better too.'

'To know me is to love me, eh?' She was joking, but the worried glance he shot her made her realise what she was saying. Of course he didn't love her. They hardly knew each other for goodness' sake. But now she'd made things awkward between them when this wasn't supposed to be anything more than a casual arrangement.

Not least because the thought had its merits.

She was beginning to wonder what it would be like to have him in her life, loving her, wanting to be with her on a long-term basis. And why that would be such a bad thing. She'd already done the hard part in letting him into her life. The thought of being part of a couple again wasn't a frightening prospect as it once had been, if it included Taylor.

He'd shown her that not all men were like Steve, capable of deceit and causing pain. There were some still out there who were honourable, and kind and might even have been hurt just as much as she had.

Perhaps, more importantly, he had helped her remember that she wasn't the one who'd done anything wrong. That she shouldn't be embarrassed by how she'd been wronged, and there was no need to punish herself by hiding away from the world. She deserved a life too. Even if it was never going to be the one she was starting to wish she had with Taylor.

Although the horror emanating from him simply by teasing him about loving her soon put a stop to that wistful daydream.

'Why don't we grab some loungers before the others hog them all.' Taylor swiftly changed the subject and directed her towards a sunbed, whilst he took another, putting a little distance between them. The playful banter, and any chance of further flirting, now put behind them.

Jo resigned herself to a quiet day at the pool after all. Perhaps it wouldn't be a bad thing for her to get back to doing her job looking after Isabelle. Then she wouldn't be fixating on Taylor and fanciful ideas that they could have anything more than they'd agreed on.

Taylor didn't know why Jo's jokey comment had thrown him so much. Only that he needed some space. Seeing her settling down on her lounger on the other side of the pool apparently wasn't far enough. Not when the sun was shining through her light top exposing the bikini she was wearing beneath and the body he'd got to know so well.

He was glad he was wearing sunglasses but was regretting the flimsy swim shorts.

Taylor lay down on his sun bed and tried to block out thoughts of Jo, but it wasn't easy. Never mind all the vivid memories of what they'd done together, but now the guilt of how his parents treated her was weighing heavy on his mind. As was her throwaway comment.

'To know me, is to love me.'

Although he'd only known her for a matter of days, he had come to care for her, and he was worried the more time they spent together the stronger his feelings might become. That wasn't what he wanted in his life. It hadn't escaped his notice that the whole reason he'd come here had faded into the background since he'd acted on his attraction towards Jo. He needed to take a step back if he intended not to repeat past mistakes.

With Imogen he'd fallen too hard, too fast, going all in and paying the ultimate price for his recklessness. He was afraid of the same thing happening again. Not because he thought every woman out there was going to fake a charitable cause and steal his money, but there was a likelihood that he'd end up with more war wounds. People had let him down time and time again. His father, and Imogen, specifically. He'd learned it was much safer for him to be on his own, keeping his heart to himself. The fact that he'd even agreed to this fling with Jo was a step out of his comfort zone, so the suggestion of more was merely asking for trouble. Especially when he was already growing closer to her.

'Hey, bro. It's not like you to put your feet up and take it easy with us mere mortals.' His stepbrother's shadow loomed over him blocking out the sun.

'Well, we're all here for a break, aren't we? I thought it was about time I had a day off.' It wasn't usually his style, but he figured he'd earned it. Last night on the beach hadn't been just about Jo cutting loose; he'd realised he did it too little, as well. His work was spurred on by guilt and sharing some of the wealth he'd taken for granted growing up. But now he was wondering if it was also driven by the need to keep his mind occupied with something other than his personal issues.

If he'd been running away from his problems and the pain of his breakup. Being with Jo had taken away some of that need to stay moving. He'd found there was some joy to be found in staying in one place when she was around. Of course she wasn't always going to be there, but since they only had a few days of this trip left perhaps it would do him some good to simply kick back for a while. Figure out his next move.

'Fair play, Tay.' Harry fist bumped him, happy with the explanation. Though Taylor knew no one needed an excuse around here to be idle. It was the order of the day as long as the money was still rolling in.

In terms of work, it was his father who did the majority of it to benefit the rest of the family. He was the one who came up with the ideas, and produced the prototypes for the tech market. Everyone else just seemed to be along for the ride. Of course Taylor felt some resentment when his mother had been left to fend for herself and his father's new family took it all for granted.

That was just one of the reasons he liked Jo. Her work ethic. She knew how to graft, and her recent experiences probably made her appreciate the good life they had out here better than most.

'And Jo's joining us too this morning, I see. That's just a coincidence I suppose?' Allegra sniffed as she walked past, catching the end of their conversation.

'There's not much else to do here, dear sister.'

'I guess...if you're not off saving the world.' Allegra flounced off, trying as always to denigrate the work he did. She was very much like his stepmother in that regard, and probably didn't think any more highly of Jo either. It shouldn't matter to him, but it did. He wanted them to see what a good person she was, that she was deserving of respect. As was he.

He'd never quite fit in to his father's new family. Probably because neither his father, nor his new wife, had made any effort to include Taylor. Both more concerned with the advantages money brought than taking time to parent him. Dumping his mother for a younger model also hadn't made the best impression on a young Taylor and he'd vowed to never be like his father. Instead, he wanted to do some good with the money and opportunities afforded to him. To atone for his family's selfishness. Especially on behalf of his mother.

Undisturbed by his siblings' arrival at the other side of the pool, Jo stood up and stripped down to her bikini before stepping into the pool. From behind his shades he watched her cute backside in the small triangle of fabric as she climbed down the ladder. Couldn't take his eyes off her as she swam lengths of the pool. And had to turn over onto his stomach when she eventually emerged from the water, smoothing down her hair, her swimwear clinging to her wet body.

As he willed away his body's natural reaction, and his lustful thoughts about his grandmother's nurse, he closed his eyes and enjoyed the feel of the sun on his skin. It wasn't often he got to appreciate the good weather in the countries he travelled to. More often than not it was an inconvenience, making his job harder than it should've been when there was no air con where he was working. Lying here, chilling out, was a novelty, and kind of nice. Despite the general hubbub of noise around him as the others made themselves comfortable around the pool, he felt himself drifting off.

Suddenly he was awakened by a scream, some shouting and a lot of splashing. He sat up and tried to focus on what was happening.

Everyone was standing around the pool with horror written all over their faces. Jo was back in the pool swimming with Allegra's partner, Bobby, seemingly unconscious in her arms. The water was turning a frightening shade of red, and he noticed a trail of blood at the side of the pool.

'Taylor! Can you give me a hand?' Jo's anguished cry was enough to spur him into action, immediately alert now.

'What happened?' Moving the others out of the way, he knelt down, and with Harry's assistance, helped haul the dead weight of his sister's unconscious boyfriend from the pool.

Allegra was wailing and crying and doing nothing of any practical nature as the rest of them worked together.

'He was messing about dive bombing into the pool. I think he slipped and hit his head on the side, knocked himself out.' It was Jo who passed on the relevant information, breathless from her effort to help get him out of the water.

'How long was he under the water?' Taylor asked, checking his pulse. He wasn't breathing and was unresponsive.

'Not long. I jumped in straight away.' She clearly hadn't even stopped to take off her cover as it clung to her like a wet second skin.

'He's not breathing. I'm going to start CPR.' Taylor's assessment was met by more wailing.

'Do you want me to give him rescue breaths?' Jo asked kneeling down beside him as he tilted the man's head back to open the airways.

'If you're happy to do that?' He knew not everyone was comfortable with that these days and he could just carry on with the chest compressions he'd started.

'Of course.' Jo waited until he'd finished pumping the man's chest, then she pinched the nose, made a tight seal over his mouth with her own, and delivered a couple of breaths.

They checked his pulse and breathing again and when there was no response, they repeated the process. At this point Taylor couldn't be sure what damage had been done, or where, when there was blood everywhere. All he knew was that they had to get him breathing again and they were lucky Jo had been able to get to him as quickly as she had.

Suddenly, their patient started coughing, water spurting out of his mouth that must have been pushed out from his lungs during the CPR. Relief-fuelled adrenaline shot through Taylor.

'Help me get him into the recovery position,' he instructed Jo, who seemed to be the only other competent person around.

'Oh, thank goodness.' Allegra stopped screaming long enough to sob over him.

'Give him some room to breathe, sis. Bobby, we just need you to lie where you are for a while. You've had an accident and I need to check you over.'

'We need towels or blankets. Something to keep him warm.' Jo directed the others into action, and credit to them, they seemed glad to have something to do.

'Can someone get my medical bag from my room? He has a head injury and I need to stop the bleeding.' Although Bobby was conscious and breathing, he still wasn't out of the woods. Taylor needed to see what else was going on.

He used one of the towels to clean away the blood on Bobby's head, while Jo tried to make Bobby comfortable with some blankets handed to her.

'Here you go.' His brother handed him his bag and he set to work trying to find the head wound.

'There's a deep laceration to the back of his skull.' Jo parted Bobby's hair matted with blood to expose the injury.

'It's going to need stitches and you should probably get checked over at the hospital to make sure you haven't anything more serious going on, Bobby.'

'I'm not going to the hospital,' he mumbled, trying to show off how big and brave he was even now.

'Yes, you are.' Allegra spoke up. The one person Bobby wouldn't dare go against.

'I can patch you up, but you might need an X-ray. At the very least they'll need to check you over. I'll see if I can get us on the plane that'll be bringing grandmother back.' Taylor set to work stitching up the deep wound once Jo had cleaned the area. Then she dressed it with some cotton and gauze to protect from any infection.

'We should probably get you inside. Do you think you can stand, Bobby?' Aware that they needed to get him warmed up, Jo encouraged him to stand again. Taylor caught him under the arm, whilst she took the other and they manoeuvred him into the villa.

After they got him settled on the sofa, Allegra fussed around plumping cushions and tucking a blanket around him.

'He's going to need a change of clothes. Something to keep him warm.'

'What's going on?' Taylor's stepmother appeared just as he was issuing more orders.

'Bobby nearly drowned…he wasn't breathing. Taylor and Jo saved his life.' Allegra spilled the details through her tears.

'Taylor?' His mother looked at him with questioning eyes, as though she didn't believe what she was hearing. Even though Bobby was sitting shivering on the sofa in a state of shock with everyone else gathered around him.

'It's true. These guys are heroes.' Harry slapped him on the back and, clearly overwhelmed by the situation, Allegra grabbed Jo into a hug. Much to her surprise.

'We do have our uses,' Taylor mumbled, gaining a smile from a bemused Jo.

'Well, in that case we're glad we had you both here with us for the New Year's Eve party.' The praise from his stepmother was unusually heartfelt and Taylor was equally as glad for Jo as himself to receive it. It was important to him that she got the respect she deserved. He didn't want to think about why. Afraid that he held some deep secret desire for her to be accepted into the family in case their relationship should ever change to something more than casual.

It was also a reminder that his time with Jo was limited and he didn't want to waste any opportunity they might have to be together.

'I'm going to take Bobby over to the mainland when the plane gets here. In the meantime, we should probably go and get cleaned up.' He nodded towards Jo who was still wet from the pool and covered in as much blood as he was.

His stepmother wrinkled up her nose. 'Yes, I think that's wise before your grandmother gets here.'

At least it gave them an excuse to leave.

'I think Bobby's going to be okay,' Jo said as they walked down the hall.

Taylor didn't know what came over him, but he was suddenly overwhelmed by the urge to kiss her. So he did. He grabbed her and kissed her hard, her little moan against his lips his reward. Perhaps it was the adrenaline from everything that had happened, the admiration he'd felt watching her at work or that feeling of being part of something rather than alone, but he wanted to be with her. At that moment, the only important thing was Jo and making the most of having her in his life for the short amount of time they had together. The look in her eyes said she wanted the same.

This was dangerous territory he knew, but he'd been feeling all sorts of new sensations since meeting her, and for once he intended to lean into them. This trip would be over all too soon and the likelihood was that he'd never get to be with her again.

'Is that offer of a shower still going?' Her voice was thick with desire, and no matter what alarm bells had been going off previously, they were drowned out by the sound of his blood rushing in his ears.

With the knowledge that everyone else was occupied elsewhere, they stumbled into his room, kissing and tearing each other's wet clothes off. Once in the shower they slowed things down, lathering each other up, washing off and making out in between. Even towelling their bodies dry seemed like part of the foreplay before they climbed into bed together. It didn't matter what part of the day it was, sleeping together seemed inevitable. What they both wanted and needed.

They made love slowly, clinging to one another as they reached that peak together. Staring into one another's eyes as they fought to recover. Today had seen a shift between his family and Jo, and Taylor couldn't help thinking that it was the same for them. The mood had changed between him and Jo too. He couldn't be sure in what way or why, but he did know it was frightening and exhilarating all at the same time. Something he was curious about exploring further if circumstances allowed.

Jo was on pins and needles waiting for Taylor to come back. He'd gone over to the mainland with Bobby to get him checked out at the hospital. He might take these flights back and forth with a pinch of salt, but she didn't. Those small planes were always on the news having crashed leaving no survivors. She was beginning to realise how much he'd come to mean to her in such a short space of time, and not just because of the amazing sex.

For two years she hadn't let another man into her life. He was special to have even got that far. Beyond that, he was someone who made her feel part of something. A team, a relationship, the world in general. She'd been closed off since her ex's betrayal, shutting out everyone and everything to focus on working to pay off the debt she'd been left with. It was possible she'd even fallen out of love with her job because it was so tied up with money and never having enough to stay afloat. Taylor had renewed a passion inside her not just for him, but for the work they did too. They made a difference to people. He made a difference to her.

'A penny for them?' Isabelle's concern broke through Jo's reverie.

'They're not worth it. Sorry. Is there anything I can get you?' She'd met her elderly charge off the small plane as Taylor and Bobby had left, but in typical style she'd refused to take to her bed. Instead, they'd been sitting out on the veranda taking in the air. Away from the pool for obvious reasons, even though Mr Stroud had already employed people to thoroughly clean the area and drain the pool.

'I want to take a trip down to the beach,' Isabelle insisted, pulling her lilac shawl around her frail shoulders.

'I'm not sure that's a good idea after the last time. Your family wouldn't be happy for me to take you back down. We've had enough drama for one day.' She doubted when the family had organised this get-together they'd envisioned as many trips to the hospital, and she didn't want to have to add any more to the itinerary.

'It's not their decision, it's mine. I've been cooped up in a tiny room for days. I need some sea air and a view. Now, if you don't mind, you're paid to take care of me, and that means keeping me happy.' Isabelle folded her hands in her lap, and lifted her feet onto the footplates on her wheelchair ready to go. Leaving Jo no option but to follow her wishes.

'Okay, on your head be it.' She didn't mean it. Of course if anything happened she would take full responsibility, but for Isabelle to be so snippy with her she must really need a walk in the fresh air.

'I trust you to keep me alive as long as is humanly possible. I heard that you and my grandson have been saving lives in abundance lately.'

As Jo pushed the wheelchair down the path to the beach, Isabelle confirmed she'd already been informed of events during her absence. Not all events, Jo hoped. Although they were on good terms, she wasn't sure how the matriarch of the family would take to her being involved with her grandson. If deep down her attitude was the same as that of her daughter-in-law, Jo didn't think she'd be too impressed by the match.

'You weren't long in catching up on the gossip.' She'd only been here for about an hour and apparently already had the rundown over the cup of tea she'd shared with her son and daughter-in-law on arrival.

'Well, it sounds as though you've certainly been busy. I heard you and Taylor were off together working on a nearby island too.' Was it Jo's imagination or did it sound as though she was fishing for information about their relationship?

'Yes. He does amazing work. I was lucky to be a part of it, even for a day.'

'He's a good boy. He'll make someone an excellent husband someday, don't you think?' There was mischief in her voice, as if she held out some hope that Jo was going to be the wife for him. Although it was a romantic fantasy so far, Jo liked the fact that Isabelle thought it feasible she could become part of the family someday.

'I'm sure he would, but I don't think it's in his plans to settle down any time soon.'

'Ah, he just needs to meet the right woman who can convince him.'

Jo's skin began to heat up at the thought that might be her, but she soon cooled down again when she realised it couldn't possibly be. After all, they hadn't agreed on anything other than a casual arrangement. Chances were that he might meet someone else on his travels who would make him want to stay in one place and never come back. The thought of how upset that would make her wasn't in keeping with the idea of a no strings situation. That was entirely her own fault. She'd thought she could keep her feelings separate from a physical relationship, but it was dawning on her that wasn't the case. She cared for him, wanted something more, but she was afraid to take that chance on him and risk having her heart broken again. Worse, he might reject the idea altogether and she'd never see him again.

'Do you really think that's true, Isabelle? That there is someone out there for all of us who can make us believe in love again? Enough to risk everything?' It seemed like too big a dream to consider after everything she'd been through.

Isabelle waited until they were down at the edge of the sea before she answered. First taking in the smell of the sea, eyes closed, face tilted up to the sun. 'Did you know I was engaged to another man before I met my husband?'

'No. I didn't.' Jo wasn't sure where this was going, since she was effectively saying there'd been more than one man for her.

Isabelle nodded sagely. 'I'd known Edgar since I was little. He came from a wealthy family, and it was always expected that we'd marry. I certainly hadn't had thoughts of meeting anyone else. I was going to settle down and have a family with him and that was that. Then John Stroud came along and blew my world apart.'

She looked at Jo with such undisguised love it almost hurt.

'What happened?'

'Not to be indiscreet, or crass, but we had such passion together I forgot that I was meant to marry Edgar. John didn't have any money then, but I couldn't let him go out of my life. So, against my family's wishes, and all common sense, I called off my engagement and married John a couple of months later. I never looked back.'

Clearly. She had a family and a fortune, everything she'd ever want at her disposal. Still, Jo couldn't help but feel for the jilted fiancé in this happy little tale. Feeling very much as though she was the Edgar in this scenario, who'd been betrayed and left behind whilst his partner had sought a better life elsewhere.

'Surely that negates the idea of there being "the one", though?'

Isabelle shook her head and took hold of Jo's hand. 'Don't you see? Until you've felt that same passion, that same overwhelming desire to be with that person, you haven't met him yet. Edgar met and married someone else too. As much as it may have hurt him at the time, we obviously weren't meant to be together. I can tell you've had your heart broken, Jo, but don't lose hope. I know being with a man isn't the be all and end all, but keep your heart open and you never know what might happen.'

Unexpected and unwelcomed tears rushed to Jo's eyes as those frail fingers gripped hers tightly before finally letting go. It was as if Isabelle knew exactly what had been going on in her absence and could tell what was in Jo's heart even though she'd been afraid to admit it to herself.

She was falling for Taylor, and if he didn't feel the same way she was inevitably going to get hurt. Either they both took the risk of being in a relationship or they had to end things now before she was in deep. It was all or nothing, with no guarantee of a happy ending. Even if Taylor was "the one", he might not want to be. So where did that leave her?

'Thanks for everything, Taylor. I don't know how I'll ever repay you.' Bobby clapped him on the back as they made their way back into the villa.

'Make a donation to charity in my name,' Taylor suggested in all seriousness, regardless that it was probably a futile ask.

'I will get right on that, buddy. Thanks again. I think I'll go and get myself a beer. Do you want one?'

'I'm good, thanks. I think I'll get an early night. I'm glad you're okay.' He left Bobby who went in search of Allegra and alcohol, not necessarily in that order.

After what seemed like an eternity of waiting in hospital corridors listening to Bobby's inane prattle about how much his trust fund was worth and his latest supercar, Taylor just wanted some down time. He also wanted to see Jo. Not for any particular reason other than today had reminded him of how much he actually enjoyed her company. It made the day so much more pleasant having someone to talk to, to work with and hopefully go to bed with at the end of the night. The only thing that had got him through the day spent with Bobby was the thought of getting back to her. It was amazing how quickly he'd accepted her as part of his every day. It should be worrying, but he was enjoying it too much to listen to those warning sirens going off somewhere in the distance. He'd had enough of being on his own, wounded and hiding from the world. Perhaps it was time to open up and let someone else into his life. He was beginning to think that by shying away from another relationship he'd been hurting, rather than protecting, himself. Failing to get close to someone as special as Jo.

With no sign of her anywhere, Taylor retreated to his room, the excitement of his return beginning to dissipate. He wondered if he was going to feel like this every time he returned to an empty bed now.

When he opened his bedroom door and found Jo lying asleep on his bed, it was like all of his Christmases come at once.

Loathed to wake her, he kicked off his shoes and eased himself onto the bed next to her. She stirred, a dreamy smile on her lips when she opened her eyes to see him. His immediate reaction was to kiss her fully awake.

'Sorry. I didn't mean to fall asleep. I just called in to see if you were back and I guess I got too comfy.'

'No problem. Although I would have come to find you the moment I came back, you know.' He was touched that she'd come to look for him at all. It proved she'd been thinking about him too. Whilst he wasn't sure what that meant for the long-term future, he was content being here with her now.

'Is Bobby okay? I have to say, your family seem to be in awe of your medical skills now. Perhaps now they've seen the evidence of it for themselves they'll appreciate you a bit more.'

'I won't hold my breath. As for Bobby, all his tests came back fine. He's going to have a nasty bump on his head, and I'll have to keep an eye on him to make sure the stitches don't get infected, but he should be fine.'

'That's good. I just wanted to be sure you both got back safely.' Jo went to sit up, but Taylor wasn't ready to lose her so soon when he'd been looking forward to spending some time with her.

'Where do you think you're going?'

She frowned. 'Back to my room. I'm sure you want to get some sleep.'

'Yeah, but that doesn't mean you have to go.' He patted the empty pillow beside him.

'Are you sure?' She eyed him with caution as though this was some sort of trick.

'Yes. I couldn't wait to get back and spend some time with you tonight. Even if it's just listening to you snore.'

'I do not snore.' She hit him on the shoulder but there was a great big smile on her face.

Taylor urged her back down onto the bed and gave a sigh of contentment when she snuggled into his side. 'I suppose it's more heavy breathing. Like a dormouse snore.'

'I do not snore.' There was less fire behind her denial as she cosied in next to him.

Even though they were fully clothed, Taylor pulled the covers over them, not wanting to disturb the comfortable moment. It was such a refreshing change to lie next to a woman in bed without any expectations. Of course, he'd enjoyed the sex too, but there was something special about simply being in one another's company.

He was aware of the dangers in believing they were a couple, but he was beginning to see the benefits of being with someone. Someone who had been hurt too, and who he didn't believe would purposely deceive him the way his ex had. Not only was he beginning to relax those unwritten rules he'd had in place for so long that meant he couldn't even consider getting involved with anyone again, but he was questioning whether he still wanted to keep moving.

Although he still wanted to help others, it would be nice to have someone to come home to at night like this. To have Jo curled up in his arms in bed; to wake up to in the morning, and lazily make love with her. All of those things he hadn't realised he'd missed, because it had all been tainted by his ex's deception. It didn't seem fair to deny himself that kind of happiness, which he was sure both of their partners had found elsewhere since.

He closed his eyes, weary and content. Dreaming about what it would be like to settle down with Jo somewhere and be happy not only at work, but also in his personal life. Was it too much to hope to have it all?

Jo watched Taylor sleep soundly next to her. She didn't have that luxury when her head was so full of worry, and her heart so full of something she was afraid to recognise. They only had a mat-

ter of days left together before the big party sig-
nalled the end of their time together. Whilst the
fireworks and celebrations were supposed to sig-
nify a new start, it was coming to mean something different to her. It would herald the start of
a new heartbreak.

She'd fallen for Taylor and it was going to be
devastating to have to smile and cheer with everyone else when she'd be miserable inside, knowing she'd be leaving him behind. How could she
have a happy New Year knowing Taylor wasn't
going to be a part of it?

She didn't want to start another chapter of her
life unhappy. Perhaps it would be better to cool
things now, and give her a little time to get used
to the idea of being on her own again. After all,
going home as part of a couple had never been on
the agenda anyway.

Lying here beside Taylor wishing for more than
a casual arrangement wasn't going to help her
process the fact that she was going to have to let
him go sooner rather than later.

Jo tried to ease herself out of bed without dis-
turbing him, but the moment her feet hit the
ground he grabbed hold of her arm.

'Where do you think you're going?' he mumbled, eyes still closed.

'I should get back to my own room so I'll be
there when your grandmother wakes.'

Taylor let go of her and rubbed at his eyes. 'Wouldn't you prefer to stay here with me and make the most of the morning?'

'Of course I would, but I have a duty to your grandmother. I have to administer her medication and check her blood pressure don't forget.'

'Well, I wouldn't want to get in the way of you doing that, but I will look forward to you coming to me tonight.' The promise of another night in Taylor's arms, coupled with the sultry look in his eyes, made Jo's stomach flip with anticipation.

Despite her decision to put some distance between them so she could get a grip on her emotions, there was always the possibility that it would only make her long for him more.

Once he was up and dressed, Taylor found himself going in search of Jo again. He had no desire to interfere in her work, but that need to be around her was all consuming. Most likely because in just a matter of days he'd be back to being on his own again. The staff, busy in the background making preparations for the big party, were a constant reminder of their time together ticking away. With each piece of bunting strung up outside, every food delivery, it was a dagger to his heart knowing the final countdown was on.

By the time he got to the dining room for breakfast it soon became obvious everyone else had already eaten and gone outside. After helping himself to some orange juice and toast, he wandered outside to take his breakfast on the veranda. Jo and his grandmother were sitting with a cup of tea, enjoying the morning air.

'Good morning,' he announced before inviting himself to sit at the table with them.

Jo glanced up, but quickly looked away again. 'We should probably get moving, Isabelle. It's not going to help your recovery by sitting in one place all day.'

She scraped her chair back and got up from her seat, leaving her tea half-drunk in her apparent hurry to get away from him. It wasn't the welcome he'd hoped for from her, and certainly didn't fit in with the way she'd been with him in the early hours of the morning. Taylor decided not to take it personally, as she was likely trying to keep up a professional façade in the presence of his grandmother.

'Jo's right. As long as you're feeling up to it, Grandmother, it will do you good to get out and about for a while.'

'Yes, Jo is going to show me some gentle yoga moves, but I fancy a change of scenery after lying in a hospital bed for days. We're going to take some exercise mats and head outdoors. I think we'll probably avoid the beach though this time.'

His grandmother had the twinkle back in her eyes as she joshed about her ordeal. Something she was able to do now that she seemed to be recovering well.

'If you can hang on for a few minutes until I finish my breakfast, maybe I could come with you.' It would be nice to spend the morning with his two favourite people in the world and re-create the day they took the picnic to the waterfall, when he'd begun to see Jo in a different light. Although, he could do without another life-or-death scenario on this trip. There had already been more than enough medical drama.

'No. Sorry. We have a schedule to keep. Isabelle needs to be back for her medication before lunch.' Jo had already taken control of his grandmother's wheelchair, and was grabbing their belongings as she began to move away.

'No problem. I can grab something later.' He took a last gulp of juice and rushed to catch up with them.

Only for a scowling Jo to turn back. 'No, Taylor. You stay here. I'm busy.'

He was stunned into silence. Frozen to the spot by her dismissal, and more than a little hurt as they left him standing on the veranda. At least his grandmother gave him a little wave, but Jo didn't even turn to look back. He hadn't meant to interfere in her work, and never intended to get in her way—just wanted to be near her. Clearly she didn't feel the same need.

Somewhat dejected, Taylor flopped back down into his seat, wondering what had just happened. He hoped it was simply a matter of Jo reminding him that she was here to do a job. However, her furrowed brow and sharp tone suggested something more was going on. As though she was purposely putting some distance between them. He couldn't help but wonder if he'd done something wrong when things had been great between them last night. Amazing in fact. He made a note to apologise when he saw her again in case interrupting her morning with his grandmother had upset her more than he'd realised.

It wasn't a pleasant feeling thinking he'd done something wrong to cause her sudden withdrawal from him. The uncertainty, and questioning himself and his behaviour, reminded him of the last days of his relationship with Imogen. Believing he hadn't measured up as a partner, just as he hadn't measured up as a son. He'd felt her distance herself from the relationship just before he'd discovered her deceit. In fact, that's what had prompted him to look into the charity further. Trying to show more interest in what she was doing in a futile attempt to bring them closer together. Instead, he'd discovered her web of lies, and the secret bank account she'd been funnelling his money into. Though he didn't imagine Jo was doing the same, he'd rather she was upfront about what had changed between them so he could stop beating himself up over it. Especially when he was beginning to hope there might be a chance to see one another after this. If that was nothing more than a pipe dream, he'd rather know now.

'Oh, I didn't realise anyone was out here.' His father hovered nearby carrying his laptop under one arm, holding a cup of coffee in his other hand.

'I can leave if you want?' Taylor was beginning to think he wasn't welcome anywhere. He supposed that's what happened when you distanced yourself emotionally and physically from people. Once upon a time it wouldn't have bothered him, but these past few days with the family, and Jo, made him realise how nice it could be to have people in his life. Flaws and all. He and his family were never going to see eye to eye, but he was probably as guilty of judging them as much as he'd accused them of judging him. Perhaps they simply needed to get reacquainted with one another and for him to get to know why they acted the way they did. He could only do that if he made time in his busy schedule to come back and see them, spend time together. There was a thought niggling away at the back of his mind that it might be nice to do that with Jo too, if she'd be interested in seeing him again. After their most recent interaction he wasn't so sure.

'No. Stay. I'm just checking some emails. I want to be sure all the food and drink will be delivered on time for the party and I'm waiting for the fireworks expert to arrive.' His father set his stuff down on the table and pulled up a chair.

Taylor thought that this was probably the ideal moment to start having some quality time with his father at least. He couldn't remember the last time they'd actually sat down together and talked. Plus, it would take his mind off Jo for a while.

'We missed you at breakfast this morning. We all wondered if you'd gone out already on one of your missions.'

Taylor smiled, unsure how much of the fact he'd slept so soundly had to do with having Jo next to him for most of the night. 'No, just overslept. I guess all the excitement finally caught up with me.'

'Yes, it's highlighted the fact that we aren't equipped for medical emergencies out here. I mean, you're not going to be here the next time your grandmother or Bobby need life-saving treatment.'

'Well, as much as I'm glad to have been here in their hour of need, I'm not planning on taking up residence permanently.' Although it would be the ideal job for someone who wanted to live in paradise, on their own for most of the year except when his father's friends and family decided to visit. That wasn't Taylor.

'So, I've decided to invest in the hospital and emergency transport from the neighbouring islands. It's going to take a lot of time and money to organise it, but I think it will benefit everyone in the long run. I'm going to make some calls this morning to get the ball rolling.' It certainly explained why his father was up so early. When he was on vacation he tended to spend half the day in bed.

'That's great, Dad. I know everyone we've met at the hospital and on the other islands will be over the moon to hear that. They're crying out for investment in the health care system here.' Regardless that the move was primarily for selfish reasons, Taylor was impressed by his father's initiative. As far as he could see everyone was a winner in this scenario. Not only could visitors here be sure of adequate medical attention in the event of an emergency, but so could the people who lived in the area permanently. It would also undoubtedly provide more jobs locally, as well as boost the economy.

Perhaps his father was beginning to come around to his way of thinking after all, if he was willing to part with some of his money for the general good. It was a start at least.

Taylor bit into his toast, feeling optimistic about the future, and other projects he might be able to get his father interested in.

'I can tell, and I appreciate and admire everything you do. You did well yesterday, son.'

'So did Jo.'

'Yes, she's a real asset. I guess your grandmother thinks so too.'

'Why's that?'

'She had me set up a zoom meeting with her solicitor back home. Something about making provisions for Jo in her will. I know, I know, I tried to talk her out of it, but she's determined. And, as she reminded me, it's her money to do with as she wishes.'

Taylor nearly choked on the orange juice he'd washed down his toast with. The toast that his stomach was now considering rejecting.

'Grandmother has put Jo in her will?' It was hard to prevent his train of thought from venturing down a very dark path.

If Jo had heard this news first it would explain why she'd been off with him this morning. He'd put it down to something he'd done, but it was possible she was feeling embarrassed, or guilty, about the fact his grandmother had made such a grand gesture.

Taylor wanted to think it was simply something she'd felt moved to do by Jo's actions on the beach in helping save her life. Treating her just like any other member of the family because they'd become so close. Anything other than that would give him real cause for concern.

'As I understand it's for a considerable amount. Of course, she didn't tell me the details, and I didn't ask, but she said she wanted Jo to be able to start her life over again.'

'What does that mean?' It sounded as though there was some information about Jo that he hadn't been privy to.

'You know, after the bankruptcy...' His father dismissed it as though a trifle, when in reality, Taylor felt as though the ground was disappearing from under him.

'No, I don't know. What are you talking about?'

'I don't know all the details. Something to do with her ex stealing from her business... Anyway, it's down to your grandmother what she does with her money. I have more important matters to deal with before we head back to England.' Apparently, his father was ready to drop the subject. Taylor, however, was not. Bankruptcy suggested she was in real financial dire straits, perhaps desperate enough to do something uncharacteristic. Like take advantage of a rich, elderly woman who'd come to think of her as family.

'Aren't you worried that's the reason Jo has become so close to Grandmother? Perhaps this whole situation has been orchestrated to achieve this very outcome. Don't forget what happened with Imogen.' Taylor's mood had darkened from the bright, happy disposition he'd started the day with. It was obvious Jo had shared her sob story with his grandmother, and everyone else it would seem, apart from him. Garnering enough sympathy, and emotionally manipulating her kind client into helping her out. It was possible she'd only opened up as much as she had to put an end to his suspicions, and it had worked. He hadn't believed that someone who seemed so vulnerable in that moment would be capable of such cruelty.

Jo had every opportunity to tell him about her financial situation when they'd shared such personal information with one another. He'd told her things he hadn't told those closest to him, he'd felt such a connection with Jo. The fact that she'd held back the information suggested she'd been trying to keep it secret from him. Because she knew he was suspicious of her motives from the very start. He'd let his heart rule over his head. Again.

'Listen, Taylor, I know Imogen hurt you, but not everyone is out for what they can get. You know Jo. She's good at her job and we all trust her very much. Don't let your past experience cloud your judgement. She's a good person.'

'I wish I could believe that...'

This was everything he was afraid was going

to happen. It was the reason he'd come out here. To prevent another con artist from getting close to the family and trying to take advantage of a vulnerable old woman. Manipulating her into doing something drastic like writing a complete stranger into her will. Except he'd let her creep into his affections and make him forget everything, save his need to be with her.

He felt naive for falling for another scam. Worse than that, he'd been starting to believe they might have had a future together. Instead, history was repeating itself. He'd opened his heart, only for someone else to take it and stomp on it. Using his weakness against not only him, but his family too. This time, however, he was going to take action before the damage was done. At least to his grandmother and her legacy. He feared it was already too late for his fragile heart.

'Taylor?'

Leaving his uneaten toast and half a glass of orange juice on the table, he got up to go in search of Jo and his grandmother to confront what had been going on behind his back.

'I think I'll go and check in with Grandmother. I want to make sure there are no long-lasting effects from her incident on the beach the other day.' Like being confused, coerced or agreeing to something she wouldn't ordinarily do.

'Thanks, son. I know I haven't been the father

you've always needed, but I'm glad you're here. Not only to save everyone's lives—' he smiled at his own lame joke '—but as part of the celebrations. Part of the family. You've made me very proud, and I promise I'm going to try and do the same for you.'

The only thing more unexpected than his father's new outlook was when he reached out to shake Taylor's hand.

'Thanks, Dad.' He didn't know what else to say, then his father pulled him into a bear hug, and he expressed his gratitude in the mutual embrace.

This trip had been a real rollercoaster of emotions, good and bad. At this moment in time, it felt as though he was at the top of the ride staring at the perilous drop ahead. Holding his breath in anticipation of the hardest part of the journey, waiting for it to be over so he could get back onto solid ground. Because he knew what he had to do.

He couldn't possibly ignore whatever arrangement Jo and his grandmother had come to in private. Not only did that mean he'd have to confront her about her motives for being here, for getting close to him and his family, but he'd be effectively ending things between them. That felt more of a punishment for him after everything they'd shared, and the hopes he'd had that it might continue into the new year.

If he couldn't trust Jo, he couldn't trust anyone.

CHAPTER NINE

As MUCH AS Jo loved her job, and Isabelle, she'd found herself wishing away the day. Once Jo got Isabelle settled for the night, she'd be free to go to Taylor. It hadn't been as easy as she'd imagined to stay away from him. Harder still when she'd seen the pained look on his face when she'd rejected his offer of company. In truth, there was nothing more she would've liked than to spend the day with him, but she was trying to get used to the idea of not having him around when she'd have to go home soon, without him. She only hoped he'd forgive her for her actions and welcome her back into his bed. After all, they only had a few nights left together. It could be a long time before she'd feel comfortable enough with anyone else to share this level of intimacy again, and she wanted to make the most of the physical connection she had with Taylor whilst she could. As long as he could forgive her for putting some emotional distance between them.

It had been a wrench for her to leave him to go

back to an empty bed of her own this morning. Goodness knew what it was going to be like when they went their separate ways for good. Unless he'd had a change of heart about keeping their casual arrangement she had to stop fantasising about a life together that was never going to happen. Working and travelling to far-flung places together and making love on the sand as the waves crashed around them...

'Is there anything else I can get you, Isabelle?' She forced herself back down to earth and tucked Taylor's grandmother into bed, making sure she had everything she needed at hand.

'I'm fine, thank you. Just glad to be out of the hospital. It's made me more grateful than ever for the life I've been given, and appreciate the family I have around me. Taylor especially. Without you and him I mightn't even be here tonight.' She gave Jo a watery smile that made her heart catch.

Jo had become very fond of the elderly woman, and she was sure the feeling was mutual. 'We both care for you, and we're glad to have you back. Now, you've got some water by the bed in case you need it. Get some sleep.'

'I think I will.' Her eyes were already beginning to close, exhaustion beginning to set in after their afternoon taking in the sea air and, afterwards, a battle of wits over cards. Certainly a more relaxing day than they'd both had of late.

'Do you want me to leave the light on?' Jo backed away to let her get some rest, her pulse already racing at the thought of what the rest of the night might have in store for her with Taylor.

Isabelle shook her head. 'I imagine I'll be out for the count soon. I need to talk to you about something important though, Jo.'

'It can wait until tomorrow. Get some rest.'

'Tomorrow,' she mumbled, before nodding off to sleep.

Jo smiled and eased the door shut. Isabelle usually didn't have a problem sleeping through the night, but she had a mobile phone on her nightstand in case of an emergency. It meant Jo was free to go and seek out Taylor without worrying she might be needed back here.

With a quick change into something more suitable for meeting her lover, Jo went to find him. Doing her best to quell the rising sense of panic over the fact he'd been visibly absent today. He hadn't appeared at any mealtimes when she and Isabelle had dined with the others, though his father had explained it away by saying they were working on 'big plans' for the future. It hadn't helped to assuage her fears when she was sure whatever those big plans were, they didn't include her. After all, neither she nor Taylor had wanted a further crossover between his family and their 'arrangement'. It was none of her business what

they were working on of course, but she was curious, and wary. Particularly because none of this
had come from Taylor himself. Instead, she was
the one seeking him.

'Taylor?' She knocked on his door, opening it
when there was no reply.

The room was empty, the curtains still open,
the bed unruffled. It appeared he hadn't been here
in some time. She checked the kitchen and dining
areas, took a stroll out on the veranda and by the
pool, but there was no sign of him. Only lounging
family members who hadn't seen him either. In
the end she walked down by the waterfalls where
they'd played in the water, using the torch on her
phone to light the way.

For a split second she wondered if he'd already
left the island. Jumped on a plane rather than have
to admit he didn't want to be with her any more.
Then she remembered all his stuff was still in
his room. Though he could afford to replace it
all with new if he chose to...

She was the one who'd thought to put some distance between them, but now she was concerned
he was nowhere in sight. If, when she'd shut herself off from him this morning, she'd caused him
half the anxiety and upset she was experiencing
now, she was sorry for it. Perhaps it was time to
stop pretending, and admit that she had feelings
for him. Feelings which weren't going to disap-

pear at the stroke of midnight on New Year's Eve. She was running out of time, and opportunities. If her hopes of something beyond this trip were to come to fruition, she had to put her heart on the line and tell him how she was feeling, and pray he felt the same. Of course, there was no guarantee he did, or would want more than this casual fling but she had to try.

Too often in the past she'd been afraid to confront the truth. Perhaps if she'd been brave enough she could've saved herself from the embarrassment of bankruptcy. If she was honest with herself there had been signs in her relationship with Steve that not all was well. She'd noticed him being more secretive when it came to his laptop or phone, hiding the screen from view. In hindsight he'd likely been moving money around between accounts, but at the time she'd convinced herself it was nothing to worry about. Just as she ignored that he'd been coming later to bed, if at all. She hadn't wanted to cause any upset and disrupt the happy life she'd built for herself. Unaware it was all a sham. Much like her childhood. Jo wondered if that was why she'd clung on to her relationship, afraid to push Steve away, because she needed stability, no matter what it cost her.

Now she wanted only to deal in truths, having had enough of secrets and lies to last a lifetime. She wasn't going to ignore her problems and hope for the best, she was going to take control. And, if Taylor decided he didn't want to be with her beyond the new year she would deal with it. Eventually.

She searched everywhere she could think of for him and, unless he was actually hiding behind the waterfall, Taylor wasn't taking a late-night dip either. There was only one last place to check, so she made her way to the beach. The lights draped around the daybeds were on, guiding her to where Taylor was sitting with a beer in his hands staring out at the ocean.

'Taylor?'

He looked up at her and frowned. 'Hey.'

Not the passionate reunion she'd been looking forward to all day.

'Rough day?' she asked, sitting down beside him, and swiping his beer for a drink.

'Help yourself,' he grumbled.

She didn't even like beer; she'd just wanted a way of breaking the ice. Something she hadn't needed to do before. Up until now they'd always fallen easily into conversation, even if it hadn't always been congenial.

'I haven't seen you all day.'

'Yeah. I've been busy helping Dad with something.' He seemed distant, couldn't quite meet her eye, and there was a distinct bristling when her hand touched his giving the beer back. And not in a good way. When they'd been trying to resist the attraction between them every accidental brush against one another had been electric, as if it could suddenly spark that passion to life. Now it felt as though he didn't want to be anywhere near her, and she didn't know what had changed. Other than spending last night cuddling, with no expectation of more. Or so she'd thought. Perhaps that had been enough to frighten him off. Too much tenderness for a man who purported to only want a physical relationship. It was a shame when it was the closest she'd been to anyone in a long time. Even her ex.

Their lives had been a whirlwind of business meetings, appointments with patients and families, always seeking work, hardly ever taking a break. In hindsight they hadn't made time for one another. It wasn't an excuse for his behaviour, nothing would ever justify the mess he'd left her in, or his betrayal. However, if they'd been closer, he might never have dreamed of doing it, of hurting her so much.

'He said you were working on a project together.'

'He wants to invest in the hospital and provide better transport links for the other islanders. It's mostly in case anything happens to any of the family again, I'm sure, but I can't turn down the offer when it would benefit so many people out here. So I've been making a few inquiries on his behalf to get the ball rolling.'

'That's fantastic. It's what you want, isn't it? For your father to do his best?' She couldn't understand why he wasn't psyched about the idea. Okay, so his father perhaps had his own best interests at heart, but it sounded as though this was going to be a public venture, not just for family use.

'Yes. Of course. It'll mean the world to people like Isaac and the other islanders.' Taylor set his beer down onto the table, his head dropped as he heaved out a sigh.

There was clearly something else bothering him. Her pulse sped up, along with her anxiety level, at the thought that it might be her. They had another couple of days on this island and if he was about to end things, it was going to make it very awkward for her to be here. Mostly because of having to face him, knowing what they'd shared, what they could have together, and knowing she wasn't enough for him either. The only consolation was that he wouldn't take her money when he ran. She didn't have any, even if he was as spiteful as her ex.

'I'm sorry about the way I acted this morning. I just wanted to be professional for your grandmother's sake.'

He suddenly turned to her. 'I know about the will.'

She could only stare at him blankly because she had no idea what he was talking about with the sudden change of subject. 'What will?'

'My grandmother's will. Don't pretend you don't know about it, Jo. Don't take me for an even bigger fool than you already have.' The vitriol with which he spat the words at her was physically wounding. He may as well have slapped her across the face.

'Isabelle? I have no idea about her will.'

Taylor tutted, and he was so tense she could feel his muscles clench beside her. 'Don't give me that. The first thing she did when she got back and spoke to you was phone her solicitor and have you added to her will.'

'I didn't know anything about that. I swear.' Under other circumstances she might have been touched by the unexpected gesture, but everything in Taylor's tone and body language suggested she was being accused of something. She wanted to be sick.

'If I know about it, I'm pretty sure you do too.'

'Honestly, Taylor, I had no idea. I never asked her to do that.' She was imploring him to believe her, knowing how that probably looked to him, but it certainly wasn't something she'd instigated. Apart from being unethical, she would never have taken a penny from any of her vulnerable clients. It was always their families she dealt with so she wouldn't be accused of anything underhand, taking advantage of those who put their trust in her. To hear Taylor basically accusing her of doing that very thing was even more devastating than if he had told her he was ending their fling.

She wasn't like Steve, or Imogen, who had contrived to steal and betray, and if Taylor thought that she was capable of that, he didn't have a high opinion of her at all. It caused a sharp pain in her heart the like of which she hadn't felt even when Steve had treated her so appallingly.

It meant he didn't know her at all, even after everything they'd been through together. For him, perhaps their relationship had been purely physical after all. When, for her, it had come to mean so much more. It was entirely her own fault for getting carried away when they'd both agreed this was never meant to be anything other than a casual fling.

'Oh, I'm sure you didn't do anything as crass as ask her outright to do that. You people are much sneakier about getting what you want. It doesn't matter the cost to the people who love and trust you the most.'

Jo was so gobsmacked she almost couldn't mount a defence. The wind literally knocked out of her lungs that he could think so little of her. It was betrayal of a different kind. A character assassination from someone she thought she'd bonded with. Someone she'd imagined sharing her life with. She'd got it all wrong again. It was becoming apparent that she couldn't trust anyone, including herself. Any fantasy that she could ever have a happy, successful relationship, was just that. Fantasy. A foolishness she should stop giving head, and heart, space to.

Eventually, almost shaking with rage, she managed to speak up. 'Taylor, are you seriously suggesting that I'm some sort of con woman? That I get close to vulnerable people to financially take advantage of them?'

'Maybe you don't even realise you're doing it. I don't know.' He shrugged. 'Have you told her about what your ex did, and what your current situation is?'

Jo didn't think she had any other option but to be honest, even though it wasn't going to help her case. 'Isabelle asked me about my past. She could tell I'd been hurt, and I told her what my ex did. It wasn't a ploy to get money from her. You have to believe me, Taylor.'

'I don't know what to believe any more.'

'Your father thinks I had something to do with this too?'

'I don't think so, but then you've charmed everyone in the family, haven't you? Just like Imogen.' Still the accusations came that she'd somehow manipulated everyone into liking her for her own gain. It was something, she supposed, that Taylor was the only one who thought so, but still, it hurt. Not least because he kept comparing her to his ex who had gone out of her way to hurt him, when all Jo was guilty of was falling for him.

'I haven't done anything, and I'll ask Isabelle to take me out of her will tomorrow. I never asked for, or expected, anything. Other than respect, which I guess I've failed at if you think I'm capable of such a despicable thing.' She got to her feet, her shock and upset threatening to bring tears. If she started crying, he'd probably think she was only trying to get his sympathy.

'Even if that's true, and you didn't coerce her into writing you into the will, you omitted to tell me the truth about your financial situation. Probably because you knew I'd already sussed you out. I should have listened to my instincts from the start.' Taylor slammed his beer bottle down, displaying his anger at the situation, even though he'd got it all terribly wrong.

'I didn't tell you because I was embarrassed. You already seemed to have such a low opinion of me, I didn't want to give you any more ammunition. I haven't done anything wrong, except being a truly awful judge of character apparently. You clearly don't trust me, and after everything you've accused me of… I don't think I'll ever get over it.' How could she when she'd taken such a huge risk in letting him get close and he was able to hurt her so badly without a shred of proof? All he had were suspicions, and residual issues from his last relationship, which he was projecting onto her. Uncaring about the damage it would cause her. Both personally and professionally.

If he thought her so untrustworthy, that she'd been doing the same to him as his ex, then they had no future together in any capacity. He clearly couldn't move on from his past, and if it was so easy for him to distrust her, he'd always find some fault with her. Jo didn't need that kind of toxicity in her life. She needed, and deserved, love and respect. Not doubt and accusations.

'In case you're in any doubt, this is over between us, Taylor.'

'I'm sorry things had to end this way.' He didn't seem very sorry, more relieved. Perhaps this was his way of getting out of committing even to continuing their casual relationship.

'Well, they didn't, but since you don't hold a very high opinion of me, yeah, this is over.'

Taylor simply gave a curt nod of his head.

'Regardless of what you think, Taylor, I'm very fond of your grandmother. And the rest of the family. I would never do anything to hurt any of them.' That had included him up until a few minutes ago.

Who was she trying to kid? She'd come to

the terrifying realisation that she'd fallen in love with him. That's what made this so excruciatingly painful.

He opened his mouth as if to say something, but stopped himself. Jo took it as her cue to walk away.

Somehow she managed to remain upright until she reached her bedroom before her legs collapsed from under her so she fell onto the bed. Feeling as though her world had crumbled around her all over again.

Taylor mightn't have stolen her money, but he'd left her in a mess all the same. He'd broken her trust just like everyone else in her life had done. She curled up, thinking about last night when she and Taylor had made love. It felt like a lifetime ago now. As though they'd been different people then. Before suspicion and distrust crept in and ruined everything.

Cocooning herself into a little hedgehog ball where no one else could get to her, hurt her, she let the tears fall.

She couldn't stay on the island seeing Taylor until the end of this trip, knowing what he thought of her. Not when she'd fallen for him, given him parts of herself she'd kept locked away for two years only to have it all thrown back in her face. Facing him for the next couple of days was a torture she couldn't put herself through when she was already hurting plenty. Never mind what the rest of the family would think of her once they heard about the will. She supposed Isabelle thought she was doing her a favour. An incredible gesture of kindness and generosity, which she was grateful for, even though she couldn't accept it. However well intentioned, far from helping to get her life back, she was now going to have to start afresh. This chapter was definitely over, and there hadn't been any happy ending.

'Morning.' Taylor greeted his father and grandmother who were taking tea on the veranda.

'It's afternoon,' his father corrected him.

He glanced at his watch for the first time and realised he'd slept through breakfast again. It was becoming a habit for someone used to surviving on just a few hours of sleep between clinics and flights. Although, last night it had been his guilty conscience keeping him awake until the birds' early morning chorus outside eventually sent him to sleep.

He didn't regret confronting Jo about the will; it would have been impossible to carry on while he harboured suspicions about her motives for being here. Especially when she appeared to have kept as many dark secrets as Imogen. All he could do was move on as usual and try and put her from his mind. If he could get through the next twenty four hours or so seeing her, and wondering how things could have been between them.

As he sat down, he could feel his father and grandmother glaring at him.

'What? I'm sorry I missed breakfast again. I had a couple of beers last night and I guess I'm just not used to it. I am on holiday.' He felt as though he had to justify his actions even though he was an adult. Probably because he was as disappointed in himself as they seemed to be with him. His grandmother was old-fashioned in her ways and preferred when they all dined together. Given a chance she would probably have them all sitting around the dining table using silver service and in formal dress. Though with his father's more laid-back approach to life he didn't think having a lie-in would have been the crime of the century.

'What did you say to Jo?' His grandmother's accusatory stare made him feel ten times worse than he already did.

He hadn't expected Jo to go running to his family and it only cemented the idea that she was up to something untoward by trying to cause friction between them.

'What has she told you?'

'Nothing. She's gone.' His father's very measured tone felt as though he was trying to hold back his anger. Taylor should have known he'd

end up the villain of the piece when he'd simply been trying to protect everyone. It was clear
they'd taken Jo's side in the matter even before
he got to have his say. She'd left him to explain
what she'd done and break their hearts.

'Your father said he told you about my will.
Jo left me a note asking me to amend it, and remove her from being a beneficiary. It doesn't take
a genius to work it out. I'm very disappointed in
you, Taylor. I didn't think you of all people would
begrudge someone less fortunate a little happiness.' It was obvious from the stricken look on
his grandmother's face that she was heartbroken
at losing Jo, but Taylor was sure it would be better for her in the long run that Jo was out of her
life. Because he felt the same. He had to keep reminding himself that it was better to deal with the
pain now than wait years down the line to find
out she wasn't the person he'd thought she was.
Just like his ex. It had been a pre-emptive move
to deal with it now before he, or the rest of the
family, got to rely on her too much.

'You don't understand…' He hated that she'd
left him in this position, having to spell out to everyone how she'd been manipulating them all, and
now that he'd caught her out she'd jumped ship.

'I understand that you upset her enough that
she packed in the middle of the night and had me
charter a plane back to the mainland first thing

this morning.' At least his father answered how she'd managed to leave, avoiding him and any more awkward conversations between them.

'That wasn't what I wanted her to do.'

'Well, that's what she did, Taylor. So I'll ask you again, what did you say to her?'

'I told her I thought she was being underhanded, getting close to Grandmother in order to have access to the family fortune.' Why did it sound so silly now that he was explaining it to his father?

'I don't know how many times I have to reiterate this, but I'm not senile. I have all my faculties, and I'm entitled to add, or remove, anyone in my will however I see fit.'

'I know, Grandmother, but these people are clever manipulators. They get close to you, spin you a sob story, and the next thing you know you're signing over your life savings to them.' He should know how easy it was to be taken in by a pretty face and an apparent heart of gold.

'In case you haven't realised, Jo is not Imogen. Do you think I didn't do a background check before hiring her? I knew all about her financial difficulties, but she's a genuine person. I knew that from the first time I met her. You know it too.' His father hit him hard with the truth.

'This isn't about my will really, is it? Jo didn't know anything about it. As it happens, neither of you are very good at hiding your feelings. I'm just sorry I got caught in the crossfire, and now I've lost someone very dear to me because you're both afraid to admit the truth.'

'What do you mean?' Taylor was trying to process everything his father, and grandmother, were saying to him. Because he knew it was all true.

However, he couldn't get over the look of betrayal on Jo's face last night, or the nagging doubt that he might have got it all wrong. Whatever the reason, or whoever Jo really was, it was too late to go back and change what had happened. He'd been looking for an excuse to push Jo away, knowing he'd got too close. That continuing a casual fling wasn't going to be enough for him, and the idea of committing himself to more was terrifying.

So, at the first hint of trouble, he'd jumped ship. The thought that she might be after the family fortune reminded him so much of Imogen it had seemed the ideal excuse to shut down all thoughts of a relationship with Jo. Then he didn't have to deal with the very real feelings he was having towards her.

However, his cowardice had hurt all of those closest to him. Especially Jo. There was nothing in her behaviour, in the woman he'd come to know, that suggested a hint of malice. So he'd had to concoct a scenario giving him a reason to call things off, knowing he was getting in too deep. Transferring all the qualities he'd missed seeing in his ex onto Jo, in a failed attempt to protect himself. It hadn't worked, because he was hurting like hell without her.

'You light up around one another. It hasn't escaped anyone's notice that you're spending more time with the family lately too and I know that's because of Jo.'

Taylor opened his mouth to refute his grandmother's allegation but knew it was the truth.

'I've known her for months and I've seen a difference in her too over these past few days. She's happy. Or she was. When she first came to work with me, I could tell she was sad. It was me who asked about her past, she never volunteered the information. She didn't tell me until she trusted me.'

Taylor thought about how quickly she'd shared her past with him, and what that must have taken. After all, he'd felt close enough to open up to Jo about his ex too. It was something he'd taken for granted, but in hindsight it showed the trust she'd put in him. By using it against her he'd betrayed that trust, though he hadn't realised that at the time. It was no wonder she'd gone. And a miracle if she'd ever talk to him again.

If she had used his past against him, to inflict unnecessary pain in order to push him away, he wouldn't stick around either. Of course she'd been too embarrassed to tell him about the bankruptcy. He'd felt the same when he'd had to tell everyone about what Imogen had done. Now he was worried he'd never get to see Jo again, to tell he was sorry, or to ask for a second chance. That thought was sufficient to make him see how deep his feelings for her really went. He was in love with her. That's what had made the whole situation so terrifying, and why he'd been in a hurry to shut it down. Admitting he loved her meant opening himself up again, leaving himself vulnerable, and he'd been too cowardly to do so. Instead, it had been easier to push her away.

'I've been an fool, haven't I?'

The silence said everything.

'If you hurry, you might catch her before her flight back to England.' His father scribbled down the details on the crossword page of his paper before tearing it out and handing it over to Taylor.

'I—I need some time to think.' He stared at the piece of paper, not knowing what he wanted at that moment, but sure this was one of the most important decisions in his life he'd ever make.

'Just don't take too long or you mightn't get another chance,' his father said, and that was exactly the problem.

Taylor walked away clutching the scrap of paper as though it was the Holy Grail; there was no more running away. He had to face up to the truth of what he felt for Jo, and what he was going to do about it. Hopefully it wasn't too late.

Jo hadn't cared that she'd had hours to wait in the airport before the next available flight back to England; she'd had to get off that island and away from Taylor. She dabbed at her eyes under her sunglasses so she wouldn't show her red-rimmed eyes to the rest of the world. Hopefully no one would notice she was a heartbroken tourist going home in disgrace.

She still couldn't quite believe it herself.

The only thing worse than having to leave Isabelle, and a job she loved, was the knowledge that Taylor thought so little of her. That he thought everything she'd ever told him, everything she'd done, had been part of some elaborate plan to inveigle herself into his grandmother's will. It would've been laughable if it wasn't so painful.

The reason it hurt her heart more than her ego was because against all of her promises to herself, she'd fallen for Taylor. She'd risked her peace of mind, only to have it shattered by another man quick to betray her.

Now she had to go home with her tail between her legs. With no job, no money, no new start. And nursing a broken heart.

The announcement over the Tannoy that her flight was now boarding prompted Jo to take her place in the queue that had now formed at the gate. With her bag and passport in hand she waited patiently to be waved through onto the plane, away from Taylor and the memories she would associate for ever with this place. She was also sure this time of year was always going to become a sad occasion for her too. New Year's Eve, which should've been a celebration, marking a fresh start, but was instead tainted with the ugly memory of Taylor's accusations and her resulting heartbreak.

She moved forward to present her boarding pass and passport, one step closer to home. Suddenly, she felt a pressure on her arm and looked up to find Taylor there beside her, his hand wrapped tightly around her wrist. She blinked, wondering if she was imagining him there. Conjuring up one last reason to stay.

'I need to talk to you, Jo.' As her vision spoke, making him real, Jo's heart leapt at the thought that he'd come after her. That he wasn't ready for it to be over either.

Then she remembered how he'd spoken to her last night. The way he'd looked at her with such utter contempt, and knew she was still trying to fool herself.

'What are you doing here, Taylor?' She quickly quashed that initial surge of excitement at seeing him, wondering if he'd come to berate her some more. After all, she'd left without saying good-bye, or even standing up for herself.

'I just wanted to talk to you. I had to pay for a last-minute flight just for the privilege.' It occurred to her that he would've had to have a ticket to get through security. Not that the expense would mean anything to him.

'Madam? Are you boarding? The other passengers are waiting.' The airline employee at the desk politely, but firmly reminded her that there were other people here besides her and Taylor. She'd almost forgotten.

Not wishing to cause a scene, she moved to one side to allow the other passengers to board, with Taylor in pursuit.

'Have you come to search my bags and make sure I didn't steal the family silver on the way out?' She couldn't help but snap at him like a wounded animal, afraid he'd come to start round two of the fight.

He flinched. 'I deserve that. I was out of order last night.'

'Yes, you do, and yes, you were. I didn't do anything to warrant that treatment from you.' Jo was trying to keep her voice strong, so he didn't know how much his words had hurt her. That might just give the game away that she'd come to think of their relationship as more than a casual holiday fling.

'I know. I'm sorry. Can I convince you to come back? Grandmother is really missing you.'

'Oh, so you're here because Isabelle is unhappy that I've left?' Emotional blackmail wasn't going to be enough to convince her to return and go through the hell of being with Taylor for the duration of the Strouds' celebrations. All she wanted to do was lock herself in her room, climb into bed and sleep until her heart stopped aching.

It wasn't fair that he was here reminding her of what they'd had, and how awfully things had ended. She would've been better off never seeing him again and being left to work through her heartbreak in peace. He was probably only here to save his own skin when his relationship with his family was strained enough without him upsetting his grandmother. Whilst Jo was sorry she'd left Isabelle without a carer, she still had her family around her. They could always hire someone else when they got home to take care of her. It wasn't going to be so easy for Jo to move on.

'No, I'm here because I'm unhappy that you left. More so because I'm the one who caused you to leave.'

Jo gulped, feeling as though her heart had just leapt into her throat with hope. But she wasn't so easily fooled. People didn't always mean what they said. Sometimes words like 'I love you', or 'I want to be with you', had expiration dates. She was worried 'I'm unhappy that you left' might be in the same category, and that was no longer enough for her. For her to consider anything other than getting on a plane home, he needed to come up with something more. Something she could believe wholeheartedly. After the way he'd spoken to her last night, she thought it was going to be too big an ask.

'What is it you want from me, Taylor? Because it seems as though no matter how much I give of myself to you, it's never going to be enough for you to trust me.' As far as she could tell nothing had changed since last night, other than her deciding not to stick around for more blame and humiliation.

He hung his head. 'I'm sorry. I can't say it enough, I know. Since Imogen, I've found it difficult to trust. That's partly the reason I came out here in the first place. When I first learned about how close my grandmother and her nurse were, I was worried that you were here for nefarious reasons.'

'So you had it in for me from day one? That explains a lot.' Jo thought back to that first night and their altercation in the kitchen, which was very reminiscent of their argument last night. Both times she'd been bewildered by his hostile attitude towards her, though it had hurt more the second time around after how close they'd become.

'Have I said I'm sorry?' His lopsided smile and big eyes were weakening her defences, but she wasn't giving in without a fight this time.

'Do you know what hurts most, Taylor? It's that we spent days working together, and sleeping together.' Despite her anger, she whispered the last bit. Not wanting everyone in the tiny airport to hear the private conversation and make assumptions about her character too.

'I know—'

'And you still thought I was only here to get written into a will that hopefully won't come into effect for years to come? You clearly don't think very highly of me, when I—I came to think a lot of you.' She barely held her cracking voice, and heart, together.

'That's the problem. I think too much about you. I can't stop thinking about you, Jo, and it scares the life out of me. I'm just waiting for something to rear its head and ruin everything. I guess when I heard about the will it was an easy out. I didn't mean to hurt you, I was trying to protect myself. I'm a selfish, thoughtless fool.'

Okay, so he seemed sincerely apologetic for his behaviour, but Jo needed to know what him being here actually meant. If he was simply trying to salve his conscience, or if he saw a future together in some capacity. Something which would bring its own problems.

'Yes, but you're my selfish, thoughtless fool.' Jo managed a smile.

'So…you'll come back with me?'

Jo thought about it, of spending New Year's celebrating with him and the family, but sooner or later they'd have to return to reality. If she didn't go now, it was going to be even harder second time around.

'I can't, Taylor. Our time together has made me realise I want more than a casual fling. If I'm going to share my life with someone, I want it to mean something. I don't think a long-distance, no strings relationship is going to work for me. If that's what you were thinking…'

'I will do whatever it takes to keep you in my life, Jo. If I learned one thing from pushing you away, it's that I don't want to be without you. I want to give us a chance too. If I have you, I don't need to keep running. Stay, and when we get back to England, I'll see about setting up there.' It was a big promise from Taylor, and she knew he wouldn't say it if he didn't mean it. Especially when he'd pushed her away last night.

Jo's head was in a spin. He was promising her the world, making a sacrifice she would never have expected, but he'd also hurt her deeply.

'Do you really mean that?'

'Yes. All I'm asking is that you come back to the island with me now. Please say yes.' Regardless that he was going all in, he wasn't even asking her for more than that now. Understanding that she'd been burned twice already, and would need time to think before committing to more.

'Madam? Are you boarding? The gate is closing.' The woman at the desk reminded her that she was supposed to be leaving, and as Jo glanced around, she could see that the room was empty of passengers now. Everyone else was on the plane and waiting for her.

Jo's head hurt as the pressure of the situation bore down on her. Having already made the difficult decision to leave, she was concerned that by staying she would open herself up to even more hurt.

'I'm sorry I pushed you away last night. The truth is, I was afraid of my feelings for you and jumped at the first excuse to put some distance between us.' Taylor pleaded his case, leaving her caught in this tug of war between her head and her heart.

'Madam?'

'I love you, Jo. It was only when I thought I was going to lose you for ever that I finally admitted that to myself. Please stay.' Taylor's public display of honesty, along with this surprising vulnerability, drew Jo closer to him than the door through which she'd been planning to make her escape.

If he was willing to make a commitment to their relationship and put everything on the line for her, moving on from his past, she had to forgive him. It was enough to persuade her to be brave too. 'I love you too, Taylor. Let's go back to the island together. Just as soon as we can figure out how to get back out of this airport...'

The beach, crowded with family and friends, the little fairy lights twinkling around the bar and daybeds, was almost as lovely as the night Jo and Taylor had spent there on their own. She'd had such a warm, welcoming response on her return; she was made to feel part of the family, and not just an employee.

Mr Stroud, and Isabelle, had insisted that she take the rest of the day off to settle back in and enjoy the New Year's Eve celebrations. She didn't know exactly what had transpired between them and Taylor in her absence, but no one had batted an eyelid when they'd come down to the beach party hand in hand.

He'd really made the effort to make her comfortable and included and as they stood on the beach with their glasses of champagne, she was looking forward to their future together.

'Ten, nine, eight...'

Mr Stroud paused the music to begin the countdown to the New Year and everyone joined in. 'Seven, six, five, four...'

Taylor turned to Jo and locked eyes on her as though they were the only people on the island. 'Three, two, one...'

A cheer went up at the same time as the very first firework. An expression of joy and excitement at the beginning of a new year. It all faded into the background as Taylor kissed her.

'Happy New Year, Jo. I hope this is just the start of our new life together, wherever it may be. I love you.'

Her heart fluttered, letting her know without doubt that he was the man she wanted to be with and maybe it was time for her to go all in too. 'I love you too, Taylor. That's why I want to travel and work with you.'

His eyes lit up as the sky filled with explosions of blues, reds and golds showering above their heads. 'Are you sure?'

Jo nodded. She'd given it a lot of thought over the past hours since coming back; she'd never felt so alive as she had working with him at the pop-up clinic. She didn't want safe any more, she wanted to follow her heart and see where it led.

'If this is the start of our new life together, I don't want either of us to compromise. It's time we stopped nursing old wounds and embrace our hopes and dreams instead. Here's to us. Happy New Year, Taylor.' She held her glass up to Taylor's. He clinked against it, then kissed her long and hard on the lips.

She knew then it didn't matter where they were, because he was her happy place.

EPILOGUE

'LET'S MAKE A run for it.' Taylor held his jacket up over his and Jo's heads and they ran out into the torrential rain.

Jo screamed as her light cotton dress was immediately soaked through, clinging to her skin. They ran the short distance from the community centre to their house. It was a dilapidated shack that Isaac and his team had renovated for them to stay in when they came back to Loloma Island. With the plans his father had implemented for the hospital and transport in the area, it was decided that Taylor would come to oversee proceedings. Of course Jo had wanted to come with him. They hadn't spent a minute apart in the six months since the New Year's party. Isaac and the others had welcomed them back with open arms when they'd suggested reopening the clinic in the meantime.

Despite the contrast between their basic amenities here, and the luxury villa on the neighbouring Bensak Island, this had become their home.

They let themselves into their little shack, only to find almost as much rain pouring in through the ceiling.

'I guess they aren't used to this much rain out here,' she said, glancing around at the puddles beginning to form on the floor.

'It won't last long. Don't worry.'

'I won't worry about anything as long as I'm with you,' Jo said, meaning every word. Nothing else seemed to matter as long as they were together. She no longer had to stress over whether or not to trust him because he'd shown her how much he loved her every second since that day in the airport.

With Taylor's support she'd even been able to reconcile with her parents before they'd left England to come back out to Loloma again. They'd returned long enough for Jo to wrap up her work commitments, and speak to her parents. After a much-needed heart to heart, they'd all got to say their piece. A lot of tears and hugs later, Jo felt as though they really had another chance at becoming a family again. They understood how upset she'd been about the truth they'd kept hidden from her, and the impact it had on her. In turn, she'd come to realise that they'd thought they were acting in her best interests, trying to protect her. Something she'd come to relate to more lately...

Taylor slid his arms around her waist and held her to him, the rain still pouring in around them.

'Marry me,' he suddenly blurted out.

'Pardon me?' It wasn't something they'd discussed, or that she'd been prepared for. Though nothing about their relationship was conventional.

'Marry me. I want to make a commitment to you.'

'You don't have to.' As much as her heart was hammering in her chest with the romance of it all, she didn't want him to feel as though this was something he had to do to make her stay with him. She knew what a big deal it was for him when the idea of a relationship at all had freaked him out not so long ago.

'I want to.' He smiled, and dropped a kiss on her lips.

'Hold that thought… I have something to tell you that might make you want to jump on the first flight out of here.' She was hoping he wouldn't, that in making a commitment to them as a couple and having a future together, that her news would be welcome. If unexpected.

'No chance.'

Jo took a deep breath. 'I'm pregnant.'

She watched with bated breath as his frown transformed into a big beautiful grin.

'We're going to have a baby?'

Jo nodded. 'We're going to be a family.'

Taylor lifted her up and spun her around. 'All

the more reason for you to say yes then. We'll be a proper family.'

'Of course it's a yes. I love you and I can't wait for us to be a little family.'

They sealed their future with a kiss, and Jo knew whether they settled here, England, or anywhere else in the world, she'd never want to be anywhere else but with Taylor.

* * * * *

*If you enjoyed this story,
check out these other great reads from
Karin Baine*

Festive Fling with the Surgeon
Midwife's One-Night Baby Surprise
An American Doctor in Ireland
A Mother for His Little Princess

All available now!

HARLEQUIN
Reader Service

Enjoyed your book?

Try the perfect subscription for Romance readers and get more great books like this delivered right to your door.

See why over 10+ million readers have tried Harlequin Reader Service.

Start with a Free Welcome Collection with free books and a gift—valued over $20.

Choose any series in print or ebook. See website for details and order today:

TryReaderService.com/subscriptions

RSBPA24R